Wedlock

By

Jonathan R. Rose

MONTAG

First Montag Press E-Book and Paperback Original Edition June 2022

Montag Press ISBN: 978-1-957010-10-6
Design © 2022 Amit Dey

Montag Press Team:

Editor: John Rak
Cover: *Arévalo_art*
Managing Director: Charlie Franco

A Montag Press Book
www.montagpress.com
Montag Press
777 Morton Street, Unit B
San Francisco CA 94129 USA

Montag Press, the burning book with the hatchet cover, the skewed word mark and the portrayal of the long-suffering fireman mascot are trademarks of Montag Press.

Printed & Digitally Originated in the United States of America
10 9 8 7 6 5 4 3 2 1

An acidic and addictive parable of a toxic marriage. Jonathan R. Rose turns a gritty lens on our quest for the perfect romance, skillfully showing just how insane society can get with its espousal of the long term relationship.

—David Massengill,
author of *Red Swarm* and *The Skin That Fits*.

Wedlock begins innocently enough: a young girl moves to the big city and meets Prince Charming, except in this fairy tale, happily ever after is a deadly illusion. A story about the dangers of patriarchy and blind acceptance of the status quo, *Wedlock* is claustrophobic, unsettling, and infuriating, in all the best ways. Rose is a master at turning the mundane into a nightmare. Wedlock might be the most "realistic" of his novels but that only makes the escalating terror more devastating.

—Alana I. Capria,
author of *Wrapped in Red* and *Mother Walked Into the Lake*

Jonathan R. Rose's feminist fable slices into the reader with the satirical razor of Angela Carter. The novel takes off like a runaway train: you think you know where it's going but you have to ride it to the end. An enthralling book with serious thought behind it. His dissection of the common masculine conceit that women must be protected is definitive. It's not about protection, it's about control. Rose is spot on in this flawlessly told story. Read it and weep for the sad plight of women, men, and marriage.

—James M Wright,
author of *Rhizome*and *The Kraken Imaginary*.

I

Holding the biggest knife in the house, Elena Corzo's mother approached a large portrait of the Virgin Mother. It was surrounded by flowers, dried fruits and burning candles. She grabbed the portrait and carefully placed it face down on the dining table before thrusting the knife into the brown sheet of paper stapled to the back of the portrait's frame. After pulling the knife out she flipped the portrait over. Cash spilled from the gaping wound. Following a gentle shake to make sure no money remained, Elena's mother flipped the portrait back over to ensure the picture of the Virgin Mother was not harmed. She then returned it to its rightful place with the flowers, dried fruits and burning candles.

"Where did you get all of that money?" Elena said.

"From the first day you said you wanted to go to university," her mother said, "I worked as much as I could, for as long as I could to save all I could, until the time was right to give it to you."

"That must have been over ten years ago."

Her mother nodded.

"But why did you put it inside of the Virgin's portrait?"

"I thought it was the only safe place in case anybody broke into the house."

Elena rushed to her mother, wrapped both of her arms around her, and squeezed.

After the embrace, both Elena and her mother returned to the table where the money rested.

"How much is it?"

"I have no idea."

Elena's mother sifted through the bills with her callused fingertips. She started counting aloud, but lost track every few seconds, huffing out her frustration every time.

Elena put her arm around her mother's shoulder.

"I'm sure it's more than enough, mom. There's no way it wouldn't be if you've been saving it for that long."

Elena's mother gathered the money, tied it up with a rubber band, and gave it to her daughter. Elena carefully accepted the money before putting it in the colorful purse her mother made for her years earlier. Her mother then told her she should leave for school as soon as possible.

"But classes don't start for another month."

"There is nothing for you here, Elena. There has never been anything for you here. I've always known that even when I didn't want to believe it."

Elena told her mother she would catch a bus to the country's capital city the following morning.

"You have no idea how happy I am for you, Elena, how proud of you I am for doing what you want to do. I know

I might not understand it, but it's what you want. It's what you've always wanted."

"Thank you, mom," Elena replied. "Without you, there is no way - no way I could have even thought about doing this, and now it's happening. I still can't believe it. Thank you so much, mom. Thank you for everything you've done for me."

"You can use the suitcase in my room. Go pack, while I make you something special to eat."

After getting the suitcase from her mother's room: black, shabby, and the only one they owned, Elena went into her bedroom, sat on her bed, and thought about what some people in her town had told her when she brought up her aspirations to study in the capital.

"If they hit you with their car, they get mad at you for being in their way."

"That city will swallow you whole."

"You won't be able to breathe."

"Why leave when everything you need is here?"

Elena gathered all of her clothes. They filled only half of the suitcase.

She looked at the mottled walls of her bedroom. They were covered with photographs of her and her mother, her and her grandmother, her and her cousins, her and her uncles, her and her aunts, and her and her friends.

Always around people, yet always alone, Elena never knew where her dreams and ambitions came from. Nobody gave them to her, yet she always had them, for as long as she could remember. Nobody else seemed to have them. It was police officer or soldier for the boys, actress or dancer for the girls.

No other options. That was it. That seemed fine to everybody else but her. Elena was scared of the policemen and terrified of the soldiers. She liked dancing, but never in front of an audience. And she never wanted to be an actress because she hated the idea of having to pretend to be somebody else when it was already so hard just being herself.

She didn't want to follow her dreams because it was exciting, because it was the right thing to do, or even because she thought she was supposed to, or had a right to. Elena was determined to follow them because she didn't have a choice. They infected her, and if she stayed in her town she thought they would consume her, torture her until she either abandoned them completely or went mad trying to grip them tighter even though they had long disappeared.

Elena was home but could no longer stay. Surrounded by all she knew, she had to flee. It was already too frustrating being embarrassed all the time, constantly feeling like an outsider, even though she looked like everybody else around her. She often wanted to cry but didn't think anybody would see her. She wanted to scream but didn't think anybody would hear her.

She didn't know why everybody around her so joyously ate the same food from the same plate, day after day. Always the same. Elena wanted more and was sick of being shunned for it, sick of being looked at with crooked eyes that glossed over whenever she tried to explain herself. Yet, with her eyes still fixated on the pictures of her and her family and friends, she knew she would still miss every single person in them, as much as she would miss the mottled walls on which they hung.

Just as she shut the suitcase, Elena's nostrils flared when the soothing aroma of her mother's cooking swept into her bedroom, knowing that it was the same meal she had loved since she was a child, *tinga*, the only dish she'd eat with onions in it. As much as she wanted to indulge in the comfort of the meal, as much as her mouth watered at the thought, as much as she knew she would enjoy every bite, she also recognized the trap it represented, which strengthened her resolve to leave even more. But before she left the room, she re-read her university acceptance letter one more time, just to make sure it was real, just to confirm that her dream was in sight, and she was finally free to chase it.

2

~

Fireworks celebrating the saint of the day exploded, smashing the eardrums of sleeping stray dogs and sending them into a state of fear and panic.

Wearing a dress her mother made her and her only pair of sandals, while holding a bag of food her mother prepared for her journey, Elena stood beside a pole with the faded picture of a bus wrapped around the top. She was finally going to board one of the buses she had seen racing through the highway that cut her town in half, rarely stopping as they made their way toward bigger and better things.

"The bus," her mother said. "It's coming. You can see it over there."

Elena saw the bus and an enormous cloud of dust following it. With her free hand, she grabbed the handle of the suitcase.

The bus slowed before stopping in front of Elena and her mother. The door opened. The driver glared at Elena.

"Ticket," he said.

Elena pulled out the ticket she purchased at the nearby shack that was a bus ticket office, restaurant, convenience store, travel agency, public washroom, and clothing store.

The driver got up from his seat, walked down a short set of steps, glanced at Elena's ticket, walked past her to the side of the bus, and opened a large door, revealing a dusty compartment filled with giant bags wrapped in frayed rope, cardboard boxes on the verge of collapse and suitcases just as worn as Elena's.

"Your bag," the driver said.

Elena handed the suitcase to the driver. He tossed it into the compartment. Elena hoped it would survive the long journey to the capital.

The driver closed the compartment door.

"Let's go," he said.

Elena looked at her mother and saw tears spilling from her eyes. She grabbed her mother and hugged her. Her mother continued to sob while telling her daughter she didn't want her to go, before telling her she had to go.

After her mother relinquished her grip, Elena approached the door of the bus. Scared to take the first step, scared to cross the threshold, she just stood there.

The driver loudly stomped his foot and exhaled impatiently.

"Come on," he said.

Elena raised her right leg and planted her foot on the first step of the bus's short staircase. She could still hear her mother weeping. She raised her left leg and planted her foot on the same step. She started to turn, anxious to offer her mother a smile before uttering words of appreciation she hoped would quell her tears, but the driver slammed the door shut, shifted the gears, and pushed the gas pedal. Elena stumbled and nearly fell.

When she regained her balance, Elena made her way up the staircase and ran to her seat at the back of the bus. She looked through the vehicle's rear window, hoping to see her town, her home, and her mother, hoping to offer a final wave goodbye, but all she could see was a thick cloud of dust.

She went to her seat, looked through her window, and saw a familiar mountain with a white summit looming ahead. Ever-present, the mountain always greeted her whenever the sky was clear. Her mother told her the mountain guarded their town.

Elena watched town after town pass by. Each one had several restaurants lined side by side, all serving the same kind of food, all open for business, all empty. Each town looked just like hers.

The mountain was getting closer, and before she knew it, the bus had made its way up, around, and down the peak. She had now traveled further from her hometown than she had ever gone before.

After several hours, the sky dimmed to a deep blue, with blotches of purple, as if it were badly bruised, moments away from blacking out. When the sky finally lost consciousness, Elena saw nothing but random flashes of blinding white light shining from the cars racing by before disappearing into the night.

When Elena woke up, it took her a few moments to realize she had even fallen asleep. She looked through the window. It was still dark outside, but she could see faint traces of light beyond the horizon.

The calm of the slowly awakening day was shattered by a caravan of military vehicles racing by, each one equipped with a machine gun mounted on the roof. Every vehicle was filled with men armed with assault rifles, helmets on their heads, and masks covering their faces, making it impossible to identify them. While Elena was used to seeing military vehicles either prowling along or racing on the highway slicing through her town, she still trembled whenever she saw them, the boys from her youth becoming the men they had little choice but to become.

After the military caravan was out of sight, Elena saw the golden lights of what she assumed was the capital. Above those lights, surrounding them, were even more lights covering the surface of what looked like a collection of peaks. She wondered if they guarded the capital just like the mountain with the white summit guarded her hometown.

After the bus rounded several curves, Elena saw an enormous patch of darkness stretching from where the bus was and where the start of the capital began.

Believing there was nothing but open land within the dark space, Elena was shocked when she started seeing buildings everywhere. They were grey and lifeless and passed by in a depressing blur. There were barely any lights, making everything seem even darker and bleaker.

The bus started picking up speed. Elena believed the vehicle felt the same discomfort she did and wanted to get through the darkness as quickly as possible. She was relieved, as the possibility of the bus breaking down terrified her. Everything about the place felt wrong. It looked predatory. If chased, there was nowhere to hide. If trapped, there was nowhere to escape. If forced to call for help, there was nobody to hear the plea.

Through the window, Elena saw a long brick wall topped with shards of glass teeth and rolled bushels of razor wire, and despite the early morning darkness and speed of the bus, due to the vibrant colors used she was able to see a collection of murals of what looked like people painted on the wall. She was unable to distinguish any details of the figures' identities, however, as they were mostly covered with missing posters of smiling children and wanted posters of scowling men.

When the bus finally left the darkness behind, Elena couldn't understand how such a grim place could precede such an illuminated city.

3

Enveloped by traffic, the bus constantly stopped and moved, jerking Elena's head forward and back every time. She looked at the other passengers occupying every other seat on the bus, almost all of whom were asleep. A woman across the aisle was snoring aggressively, her mouth gaping open. Elena wanted to wake her up, partly to stop her awful snoring, but also to ask her how she could sleep so intensely through such chaos. She looked around and considered asking the same question to a man who was awake, but when she glanced in his direction the smile he offered made her queasy.

When the flow of traffic loosened, and the bus's speed increased, Elena gasped when it made its way up toward the sky. She grabbed the armrest of her seat and squeezed. Terrified to look through the window, but overcome with a need to see, she turned her head and immediately regretted it. The bus raced along a bridge aimed straight up until it reached a curve that looped around at top speed, allowing Elena to look over the edge. Her eyes bulged when she gazed at the city spread out beneath her. It seemed to go on forever.

As the bus made its way down the bridge into the city, Elena's heart beat faster. Her fingers twitched. Her toes clenched. She saw people walking in every direction, cars constantly turning, trains zooming by on tracks she didn't even know were there and tin-topped buses bullying their way through crowded avenues. Everything in the city was moving, as if it was a living being, constantly breathing, relentlessly functioning.

After an array of turns, stops, and at least a half-dozen near collisions, the bus finally made its way into the station. It was enormous. Elena pressed her face against the window, staring at the dozens of buses parked in their allotted spaces, some letting passengers out, others welcoming passengers in. She wondered where the people getting on the buses were going, and where the people getting off were coming from.

As soon as her bus stopped in its allocated space, every single passenger jumped from their seat and huddled into the aisle, except for Elena, who remained seated, staring through the window, amazed at the number of people outside. Nobody in the aisle moved forward. After a few seconds, still standing there, jammed up like the cars in traffic, many of the passengers started grumbling. Several tense moments passed before they were finally permitted to exit the vehicle.

Elena was the only person left on the bus. She stood, looked ahead, and saw the driver standing up from his seat. He was putting on a thin jacket. He turned and looked at her.

"What are you waiting for?" he asked.

"It's my first time in the city."

"Good luck," he replied before exiting the bus.

She made her way down the aisle, scaled the steps of the short staircase, and walked out of the bus. She heard vehicles grunting, people shouting, babies crying, and immediately felt as if she was gifted the power to read people's minds only to be cursed with having to hear all of their thoughts at the same time.

The fumes from the buses starting their engines, the caked sweat of the people lugging bags bigger than them, and the food eaten by everybody around her created a stench potent enough to make her eyes water. She started to choke. It took several hoarse coughs before she finally managed to clear her throat.

After grabbing her suitcase from the opened compartment at the side of the bus, Elena passed through the doors leading into the massive station. Unsure where to go, she looked around, spotted a taxi stand, made her way toward the long line-up of people in front of it, and waited until it was her turn.

"Where to?" a woman seated inside of a booth surrounded by glass said.

"I just got here," Elena said, "and I'm not sure where the best place to stay in the city is."

"Where to?" the woman repeated.

Feeling hot breath against the back of her neck, Elena turned around. Scowling, exhausted-looking people stared back at her, all of whom had luggage held in their hands or resting against their legs. Elena turned back toward the woman gazing down at her from inside the booth.

"I'm sorry. I don't mean to hold up the line, but I just need a little help. I'm starting university soon, and--"

"Listen," the woman said, "If you don't know where you're going, I can't help you."

Feeling the breath against the back of her neck grow harsher, Elena retreated from the line. During her escape, somebody within the line extended their hand, catching her attention. It was a young man.

"You should go to the city center," he said. "There are a lot of hotels around there."

Elena smiled, thanked him, and went to the back of the line. When it was finally her turn, she looked up at the booth and the woman seated inside.

"Where to?" the woman said.

"The city center."

The woman printed out a ticket and told Elena the cost of the ride. Elena reached into her purse and stripped away some money from the tightly bound cash her mother gave her.

"Go over there," the woman said, pointing her finger toward another lineup of people.

"Okay," Elena replied. "Thank you very much. I'm sorry for holding things up before, but--"

"Where to," the woman said to the person waiting behind Elena.

With her ticket in hand, Elena walked over to the next line-up of people she was directed to. She waited until a man gestured for her to get into the taxi that had just pulled up. Before she could say anything, the man grabbed and tossed her suitcase into the trunk of the car and approached the next person in line. After Elena got into the car, the driver glanced at the ticket she handed him and drove off.

As the taxi driver weaved through traffic, constantly swearing and honking his horn, Elena stared through the window, trying to absorb everything passing her by, but it was impossible. There was way too much, moving way too fast.

When the taxi arrived at the center of the city, Elena stepped out of the car and immediately had to jump back inside when another car almost hit her. When she looked up, the driver was staring down at her, holding her suitcase, smirking.

"You should be more careful," he said.

Elena got out of the taxi, but this time looked both ways, before nodding at the driver, taking her suitcase, and making her way to the sidewalk. As the taxi pulled away, another car pulled up beside her but did not stop. The car followed her as she walked, while the driver honked his horn and whistled at her before driving away.

She turned and walked into an enormous square. Surrounded by people, she looked up and saw the nation's flag flapping in the wind. It was the biggest flag she had ever seen.

Trying to make her way through the square, Elena could hear and feel her suitcase bouncing up and down. The pavement beneath her feet was uneven, wreaking havoc on the already stripped wheels of the shoddy piece of luggage. She stopped, knowing she could not continue aimlessly walking around, knowing the suitcase would not be able to endure much more.

She was amazed by the sheer amount of people moving throughout the square and hoped at least one person would help her find a place to stay. She tried to ask a woman walking toward her for assistance, but the woman, despite Elena's best efforts to get her attention, just kept walking. She repeated the process several times, but every single time people just passed her by, as if she wasn't there.

When she finally did get somebody's attention, a young man, whose facial expression made her uncomfortable the moment he stopped and smiled at her, told her she could stay with him at his house.

"No, thank you," she said.

The young man shrugged and walked off.

She left the square, sat on a nearby bench, caught her breath, looked up, and saw a large sign that read: Hostel.

Unsure what a hostel was, she figured the word was close enough to hotel to warrant a look. She got up from the bench and walked toward the building, dragging her suitcase behind her. When she walked inside, she was welcomed by a young woman sitting behind a large desk. The woman smiled and asked Elena if she needed help.

"I'm looking for a place to stay for a while."

"How long?" the woman asked.

"I'm not exactly sure," Elena replied. "I'm attending university next month."

"We offer private rooms at affordable weekly rates."

Elena nodded.

"The washrooms and showers are shared though. Is that okay?"

"That's fine," Elena said, "I've always shared a washroom."

Elena asked how much the room was. The woman told her the price. Elena said she'd take it, reached into her purse, and thinned out the bound collection of cash her mother gave her even more.

"Your room is on the second floor," the woman said after handing Elena a key. "If you need towels, you can rent them from me or whoever is at the desk."

Elena thanked the woman and made her way up the stairs. Once she reached the second floor, she found her room. It was small. The air was moist. There were rust-colored blotches on the walls. The window was shut. After placing her suitcase next to the bed, Elena walked to the window, hoping to open it, poke her head out and view the city's square, but the window would not budge, and four iron bars distorted her view through the glass. She went back to the bed, sat on the edge, and fell backward. The mattress was stiff, and the pillow was lumpy. She couldn't have been happier.

4

Anxious to explore, Elena didn't bother showering. She didn't bother changing her clothes either.

When she reached the receptionist's desk, she asked the young woman sitting behind it what the best way to get to the university was.

"The subway," the woman said. "There's a station a couple of minutes from here. Just cut through the main square. It's right there. You can't miss it."

"Which station do I get off to get to the university?"

"University Station."

Elena tried to mask her embarrassment with laughter and was relieved when it was not only accepted but embraced by the other woman's comforting smile.

It was hot outside and the deeper she immersed herself within the crowd occupying the square the hotter it got. Elena started to sweat. Her dress stuck to her body, fastening itself to her hips and chest like a second skin. She noticed several men staring at her, pointing and smiling. She walked faster, trying to escape the crowd.

When Elena finally reached the entrance to the subway station, she walked down the steps and almost fell when one of her sandals slipped off her foot. After regaining her balance and putting her sandal back on, she scaled the remaining steps and spotted a man slumped on the floor. Old with no shoes, his dark complexion was similar to hers. He raised his empty hands. She reached into her purse and dug for coins. However, she was constantly forced to pull her hands out just to maintain her balance as she was continually bumped into and shoved by the never-ending flow of people. After getting struck in the stomach by a huge cardboard box, she abandoned her attempt at finding coins for the sake of her safety and walked away, leaving the old man and his empty hands behind.

The station was stuffed with people. More sweat bubbled from Elena's skin, soaking her body even more. Desperate to find a place to cool off, she looked around and saw a large fan. She rushed toward it, pushing and shoving her way through the crowd.

She found relief underneath the fan. It not only blew cold air but also refreshing mist that cooled her hair, face, and body. She stood there for several minutes, waiting until the last drop of sweat had been extinguished.

As soon as Elena stepped away from the fan's cold breath she was immediately swallowed by the crowd. The sweat returned. Salty droplets slipped from her brow and struck her eyes, stinging them.

When she reached a set of turnstiles, she asked a police officer standing in front of them what she was supposed to do.

The disinterested officer looked at her, grunted, and pointed at a long line-up of people waiting in front of a booth with a sign above that read, tickets.

When it was finally her turn, Elena asked the person sitting behind a severely smudged window how much it cost for a single trip. After she was told the price, she paid and received her ticket.

Once again forced to push her way through the crowd, she made her way down another flight of stairs until she stood on a platform filled with so many people she was surprised nobody fell onto the tracks. There were no fans and no escape. She felt as disgusting as the stench wafting throughout the platform.

In an attempt to take her mind away from the suffocation of the crowd, Elena spotted a large map of the city's subway system on a nearby wall. There were several lines crisscrossing throughout the map. Each line was a different color, from red, green, orange, and purple, to yellow, blue, pink, and brown. Each line had several circles indicating a station. She tried to count them, but there were too many.

After turning back around, she noticed all of the women on the platform were wearing pants and either long-sleeved shirts or sweaters. Some were even wearing jackets. She couldn't understand how they didn't pass out from heat stroke, or how the sweat she believed had to be covering their bodies underneath their layers of clothing didn't drive them crazy.

When the metallic train finally arrived and violently came to a screeching halt, Elena jumped back, eliciting a giggle from a small group of children standing behind her. The doors opened. Waves of people poured out and overwhelmed her, pushing her back, while the crowd of people behind her pushed her forward, trying to force their way into the doorway, trapping her in between. Unable to oppose either side, Elena went limp and allowed the momentum of those trying to board the train to propel her inside. Once inside, she miraculously managed to secure a seat.

The seat had no cushioning, only cold metal. It was uncomfortable, and as soon as the train started moving, she had to constantly shift her position just to avoid slipping off.

The train left the station. Elena looked around and saw people's heads constantly drooping before abruptly rising just to fall and rise again, while others refused to resist and succumbed to sleep. She saw people kissing each other passionately, not caring who was watching. She saw people arguing with each other, yelling at the top of their lungs, trying to be heard over the sound of other people shouting at them to be quiet. She saw people ignoring everything in favor of the music playing in their headphones. She saw women flawlessly applying their make-up, despite the train's constant jerking. She saw a young girl stand and take off her jacket, revealing a white t-shirt drenched with sweat, before sitting back down. Several men leered at her and the girl put her jacket back on. She saw police officers standing by the doors, looking bored. She saw people listlessly gazing through the windows. She saw people with spiked, brightly colored hair. She saw people with no hair, their bald heads reflecting the dim lights flickering above.

She saw a man dressed up as a clown, yelling out jokes at a rapid pace, trying to garner a reaction. And with every giggle and chuckle he caused, he rushed to the source, demanding payment for the joy.

After the clown made his way to the next car, the train suddenly stopped. Elena looked through one of the windows. All she could see was grey concrete.

She closed her eyes, thinking about the university, recalling the images from the brochure she received along with her acceptance letter. She wondered what it would feel like walking through the enormous grassy fields surrounding the school's faculty buildings. She wondered what the food inside of the cafeteria would taste like. She wondered what the desks within the classrooms would feel like. She wondered how the teachers would address her. She wondered how her classmates would treat her.

The train came back to life, but only for a second before stopping yet again, much to the loud dismay of everybody inside.

She opened her eyes. Her body stiffened at the sound of a crash. Unsure what was going on, she looked at the faces of the people seated across from her and beside her. All of their eyes were pointed at the floor. She looked down the aisle and saw a young, shirtless man standing above a blanket covered with shards of broken glass.

The young man's body was covered with scars, some old and badly healed, others fresh and still bleeding. His hair was a mess with bald patches scattered throughout. His eyes were glazed. His face was pockmarked.

The young man stared at the shards of glass, looked up at the people refusing to look back at him, turned, and fell atop the bed of shattered crystal. The crunching and snapping of the glass were soon overshadowed by the sound of the man groaning in pain. Yet, despite the agony he was suffering, he remained on the shards and even started rolling his body on top of them. He paused and raised himself just high enough to show the new wounds he had just suffered. He rotated his body to the side before slamming his horrifically scarred shoulder into the broken glass, over and over and over.

"Change," he said. "Please, change, can anybody give me change?"

Elena gasped. She was the only one. Nobody else even looked up from the floor. With the man continuously slamming his battered body against the shards of glass, Elena kept staring. After what she hoped was the final collision between the young man's body and the bed he had made for himself, the man sat straight, staring at those who refused to look back. It didn't take long before his eyes caught Elena's. She tried to look away, but it was too late. The man stood. Leaving his painful bed behind, he walked down the aisle and addressed each person directly, asking them for help, but they all refused to look up. Furthering his progress down the aisle, the young man constantly glanced at Elena, whose eyes remained focused on his broken body.

When he finally reached her, the broken man smiled and knelt forward. She looked into his eyes. They were dilated. He opened his mouth. His breath was foul. His teeth were yellow, some were even black. He mumbled something she couldn't understand. She looked around, hoping somebody would see what was happening and save her, but all of the other passenger's eyes remained focused on the floor.

Unsure how to respond, she nodded nervously. The man leaned closer. Not wanting to smell his breath any longer, not wanting to see the grotesque smile on his face, she tried to look around, but he was so close she was unable to see anything but his mutilated body. His wounds were sickening. Some of them showed signs of infection. Others appeared completely rotten, while the freshest ones pulsated as blood leaked from them. She was barely able to stop herself from vomiting on the man's filthy bare feet.

Hoping the encounter would soon end, Elena noticed the man extend his hand, exposing his empty palm. She looked up.

With the broken young man showing no signs of leaving, Elena noticed drops of blood from one of his wounds falling and splashing on the floor, near her exposed toes. She reached into her purse. When she felt the cold, coarse surface of a coin, she grabbed it, pulled it out, and dropped it into the man's palm.

The man looked down at the coin, closed his palm, smiled, and nodded before continuing down the aisle, where he was met with downcast eyes and silence.

After the broken man reached the end of the aisle he turned around and returned to the bed of broken glass. He pushed the pieces of glass to the center of the opened blanket, creating a mound. He then grabbed the corners of the blanket and closed it, swallowing every shard. He lifted the makeshift sack and walked back down the aisle. After he passed Elena, she watched him walk until he stopped at the beginning of the next train car, where he dropped the sack, creating the same crash she heard earlier. He once again exposed the shards of glass for none to see, as all of the passengers stared down at the floor.

The train finally started moving again. Looking up at one of the many maps lining the upper portion of the train car, Elena counted ten more stations until she reached her destination.

She looked to her right and saw an old blind man awkwardly walking down the aisle, using a stick for guidance, while asking for change. She looked to her left and saw a younger man, leaning against one of the doors, singing loudly. His voice was awful. Elena looked at his hand waving wildly and noticed he had a long, dirty pinky nail. After finishing his song, the young man pulled out an inhaler and sucked on it before launching into another terrible rendition of a song she remembered from her childhood.

With only eight stations to go, Elena saw a little girl handing tiny pieces of paper to any passengers willing to accept them, dropping them onto the laps of those who wouldn't. When the little girl reached Elena, she accepted the piece of paper and looked at the girl's face. The child's skin was as dark as hers. She looked down. The child was barefoot. Elena smiled at the girl. The girl did not smile back.

Elena read what was written on the tiny piece of paper. There were only four sentences, typed in capital letters, rife with grammatical errors.

HELLO, I'M SORY TO BOTHER YOU FRIENDS.
I DON'T SPEAK YOUR LANGUAGE VERY WELL,
ONLY THE LANGUAGE OF MY PEPLE. WHERE
I COME FROM THERE IS NO WORK AND SUM-
TIMES I DONT HAVE FOOD. COULD YOU PLEASE
GIVE ME SUMTHING FROM YOUR HEART, FOOD
OR CHANGE, THANK YOU AND MAY GOD BLES
YOU.

The girl's name was not mentioned.

The little girl walked back down the aisle of the car and
collected the pieces of paper from the passengers who handed
them back. When the girl reached Elena, she dug into her
purse, felt for a coin, found it, and along with the tiny piece of
paper, handed it to the girl. The girl thanked her and moved
on to the next passenger, and the next one, and the next one,
until she was on the other side of the car. The only other person to give the child money was an old woman who looked
just as impoverished as she did. Awaiting the little girl at the
other side of the car was a woman, short and chubby, holding a baby close to her breast. She too had dark skin and was
barefoot.

With only six stations to go, Elena couldn't stop thinking about the little girl and the baby held in the arms of the
woman she assumed was the mother to both. The mother
looked just like her mother, while the little girl looked like
just like she did when she was a child.

After the train stopped at a station, which she assumed was
popular since a surge of people both departed and boarded the
train at the same time, Elena heard several people throughout

the car yelling. All of them were selling things they held in their hands, kept in a box, had slung over their shoulders, or had dangling from the inside of their jackets.

By the time the train reached the next station, more people anxiously trying to sell whatever was in their possession came aboard, turning the train into a bustling market. All Elena could hear were voices shouting out the names of the items they sold and the prices from which they could be purchased. It was always one thing at a time, however, as there appeared to be respectful camaraderie between the vendors.

They sold books for children. They sold books for adults. They sold candy in boxes. They sold candies individually wrapped in plastic. They sold bottles of water. They sold socks. They sold umbrellas. They sold disposable raincoats. They sold lighters. They sold flashlights. They sold batteries. They sold miniature maps of the world. They sold miniature maps of the country. They sold miniature maps of the city. They sold small rubber balls they bounced on the ground to the amazement of gazing children. They sold USB keys filled with pirated songs. They sold nail clippers people purchased and used right then and there. They sold pocketknives. They sold screw drivers. They gave away pamphlets about the glory of God. They sold lint removers. They sold shoelaces. They sold individual postcards of beautiful, foreign places. They sold books of a dozen postcards of beautiful, foreign places. They sold nail polish. They sold nail polish remover. They sold lipstick. They sold mascara. They sold foundations. They sold blush. They sold eyeliner. They sold tweezers. They sold pressed powder. They sold personal mirrors. They sold deodorant. They sold toothbrushes. They sold toothpaste. They sold hand sanitizer. They sold earphones. They sold earplugs. They sold sleeping masks. They sold packages of tissue paper. They sold masking tape. They sold duct tape. They sold scotch tape. They sold liquid glue. They sold glue sticks. They sold pens. They sold white out. They sold pencils. They sold erasers. They gave away anti-government pamphlets. They gave away pro-government pamphlets. They sold handmade pieces of art. They sold hand cream. They sold foot cream. They sold baby wipes. They sold scissors. They sold razor blades. They sold hair ties. They sold hair clips. They sold Bobby pins. They sold rubber gloves. And they sold squeezable stress balls, which Elena considered buying, but was unable to because the vendor got off the train before she had the chance.

With one station to go, Elena heard music blasting out of a speaker poking out of the bottom half of a knapsack worn by a young man with tattoos covering every inch of his exposed skin. No more than the first few seconds of one song played before the first few seconds of another song started playing. The volume was way up. It was so loud Elena could no longer hear the shouting of the vendors constantly moving up and down the train's aisles.

With a headache pummeling the inside of her skull, she hoped the train would soon arrive at her destination, but to her horror, the train started to slow before coming to a complete stop. She looked through the window and all she could see was grey concrete. Trapped in the middle of a tunnel, enduring the blasting music, Elena lowered her head and stared at the floor just like everybody else.

The train rumbled to life. It picked up speed, just before slowing down again. Fearing the worst, ready to scream, she looked through the window, and to her relief she no longer saw grey concrete, but a platform, similar to the ones she had seen at the previous stations. The one difference was the giant sign that read, University. Relief. When the train came to a complete stop, she stood and made her way toward the door. Somebody immediately swooped in and claimed her seat.

Standing in front of the door, looking through a small window, she saw a crowd of people on the other side. Wide-eyed and anxious to board, the people were huddled together, ready to stampede onto the train. When the door opened with a creak and a slam, Elena took a quick breath and tried to step out, but the crowd of people on the platform refused to make room for her, or anybody else hoping to escape the train. She found herself in the same position as when she first boarded the train: trapped between two opposing sides. She turned her body, raised her arms and purse, and thinned herself as much as she could to find a seam to squeeze through. Afraid the door would not remain open much longer, she pushed her way through the crowd. Her efforts were initially weak and restrained but became more powerful and determined before making way for reckless, violent shoving. She nearly bowled over the same elderly woman who gave money to the barefoot child. Ashamed, Elena backed off, yet as a consequence of her reluctance, a woman shoved her in the back to get by, nearly sending her to the floor.

Just as she breached the invisible barrier separating the train from the platform, Elena felt a hand grab, grip, and squeeze her hip. The hand was large and strong. She had become immediately accustomed to the pushes and shoves, but this was different. This was intentional. The hand started to explore her lower body. Feeling a combination of fear, shame, anger, panic, insecurity, and disgust, she spun around hoping to see the face of the person responsible, but her attempt to identify the culprit was unsuccessful because just as she turned around, the hand was removed. She stopped and tried to spot a guilty face amongst the crowd, but only saw faces filled with annoyance, as her momentary investigation into the identity of the person who fondled her inconvenienced the crowd.

Realizing she was never going to identify the culprit, Elena moved under the will of the mob and made her way through the bowels of University Station. It wasn't until she came upon several exits that the crowd finally showed signs of relinquishing its grip on her.

She found a wall and leaned against it. She looked down at her dress and cringed at the sweat stains. She lowered her head, smelled herself, and immediately regretted her earlier decision to forgo showering in favor of starting her journey as early as possible.

Waiting for the last traces of the crowd to vacate the station, she stared at the exit. She knew what awaited her. But her excitement at finally seeing what she so passionately talked about with her mother, or anybody else willing to listen, was mitigated by exhaustion and the overwhelming desire to sleep.

5

Elena marveled at the gorgeous and elaborate mural painted on the face of her faculty building. She ran toward it. She couldn't wait to walk through its hallways, to scale its steps, to sit on its chairs, its benches, its desks. She couldn't wait to study, learn, plan, to dream within the welcoming embrace of its walls.

When she reached the building's front doors, she grabbed one of the handles and jiggled it, but it wouldn't budge. Backing away, staring at the building, she smiled, knowing she would only have to wait a few more weeks until the doors would open, and she would finally be allowed inside.

The university campus was an open oasis within a smothering city, but Elena didn't know what to do or where to go. All she knew was she didn't want to leave. It felt comfortable. It felt right. She also dreaded having to return to the subway.

Elena felt her stomach grumble. After several twists and turns through the empty campus, where she saw several other faculty buildings, along with a stadium and a collection of beautiful sculptures, she found a small restaurant. To both her surprise and relief it was open. She looked at the menu. She wasn't overly excited about any of the items available, so she settled on the least expensive one, along with a soda to wash it down.

Standing and waiting for her food, she gazed at the campus grounds, so full of green, knowing she would stay there from morning to night, every day, once the school year started.

When the food was finally served on a plastic tray, Elena paid, once again stripping away more cash from what her mother gave her, and walked to a nearby table. After she finished eating, she was about to get up when she saw two girls, each holding a tray with a plate of food, walking toward her.

With smiles on their faces, the girls came closer.

"Hi," one of the girls said.

Elena nodded and said hello back.

"My name is Ana," the girl said, "and this is Maria."

Ana and Maria sat. Elena was about to introduce herself when Ana cut her off and said, "You're not from here, are you?"

"No. I'm from--"

"No, no, let me guess. I want to guess," Ana said. "You're from the South, right?"

Elena nodded.

Maria leaned toward Elena as if she spotted a blemish she couldn't turn away from and flashed a half-smile.

"But you're so pretty. In a different kind of way."

Not sure what Maria meant by that, Elena just smiled.

"Every girl I've seen from the South, with skin as dark as yours, was always ugly."

Elena turned her attention to Ana who started intensely looking her up and down

"How much did you pay for that dress? I've never seen one like that before. It must have been really expensive."

"My mother made it for me."

"Guys here are going to like you," Maria said.

Ana nodded before adding, "And if you fixed a few things, they'd love you."

Elena asked if they have lived in the city their whole lives.

Ana said yes.

Maria nodded.

"This is just my second day, so I'm still trying to figure it out," Elena said.

"Don't worry," Ana said. "Just as long as you know where to go and where not to go, you'll be okay. There have been a few times where we've ended up in sections we shouldn't have been, but we made it out alive."

"Even though I thought we were going to get raped and killed," Maria said. "I still remember seeing a couple of ugly guys staring at us, smiling. They were dark, like you, and I thought that was it, but once we made it out, I thought it was kind of cool. It was like an adventure - like being in a different world. I felt like a foreigner in another country."

"Or a tourist in a zoo," Ana added.

Elena smiled before adding a disingenuous giggle.

"Hey, later tonight we're going out to a club. Do you want to come with us?" Maria asked.

"How would I get there?" Elena replied, her mind racing as to what she was getting herself into, and why she was getting herself into it.

"Where are you staying?" Ana said.

"In a hostel, by the city's main square."

Ana gasped.

Maria covered her mouth with her hand. She looked like she was going to run away screaming.

"You couldn't pay me to stay anywhere near there," Ana said.

Despite being fully clothed Elena suddenly started feeling the uncomfortable chill of nakedness. She crossed her arms, but it was in vain.

"We can pick you up," Maria said.

Ana turned to her friend and said, "We can?"

Maria nodded, before replying, "It's not like we're going to get out of the car, Ana. We'll just figure out a place and time, and we'll get there and pick up ... sorry, I don't think you told us your name."

Elena uncrossed her arms and smiled before revealing her name. She wanted to say more, just to feel like she was a part of the conversation, just to feel like she was there. She even raised her hand to show she had something to say, but just as she started to mouth new words Maria said, "We'll pick up Elena and go to the club."

"What time should we get her?" Ana asked.

"The club isn't worth going to until at least midnight, so how about we pick her up around eleven-thirty?"

"Where should we get her?"

"It's been a long time since I've been to the square, but I know the big, old cathedral is still there, so how about in front of that?"

"Perfect," Ana said. "We'll be in front of the cathedral at eleven-thirty."

Elena was so overwhelmed by how quickly plans were made about what she was going to do, where she was going to be, and when she was going to be there, that her hand was still raised, despite forgetting what she was going to say. After regaining her senses, she asked Ana if it was safe to be out in the square at that time.

"You'll be fine. Just don't get there too early. We'll be there at eleven-thirty exactly. I'll make sure the driver isn't late. Oh, and do you have any more of those pretty dresses your mom made for you, like the one you're wearing now?"

Elena smiled, looked down at the dress she adored, feeling good that others liked it, and said she did.

"You should wear one tonight. I like the one you're wearing, but I can see all of the sweat stains. If the other dresses you have look anything like it and are clean, wear one of those."

"And bring that colorful purse, too," Maria said. "You'll look like a real Indian; except you'd be pretty."

⚜

Standing in front of the cathedral, Elena looked at her watch, a cheap time piece her mother gave her many years ago. It read eleven-thirty-nine.

The thick crowds she had seen earlier in the day had thinned out. Their absence made the square appear even bigger than before, but it was draped in darkness, so the few people she did see walking around looked like aimlessly wandering spirits. Debating how much longer she was going to stand waiting, as she started noticing more and more of the spirits stopping to stare at her, a car abruptly pulled up in front of her. Unsure what was going to happen next, she breathed a sigh of relief when the rear window lowered and she saw Ana's face, immediately followed by Maria's.

"I love your dress," Maria said.

"Did your mom make that one, too?" Ana asked.

Elena said yes.

Maria opened the car door and gestured for Elena to get inside.

After Elena closed the door behind her, Ana ordered the driver to leave after making it abundantly clear she didn't want to spend a single second longer in the square than was necessary.

With the car escaping the darkness of the square, Elena looked at her new friends and noticed their faces appeared much whiter than she remembered.

Maria stared at Elena.

"No make-up?" she asked.

Elena said no, saying she never wore any, hoping she wouldn't be asked why, knowing she would have to say it was because she could never afford it.

As if she was about to strike her in the face, Maria leaned forward and thrust her fingertip against Elena's lips. Elena froze.

"Don't worry," Maria said, "I'm just applying some lip gloss. It will make your lips shine."

Despite how uncomfortable the gloss felt on her lips, and how badly she wanted to wipe it off, Elena thanked Maria for applying it.

"Oh God," Ana said abruptly.

"What's the problem?" Maria said.

"She's wearing sandals."

"It's fine. They won't care. It would be different if she was fat and ugly."

Elena sat quiet, nervously looking down at the exposed skin of her feet.

The car came to a sudden stop. It started again, only to stop again a few seconds later. This process of constant stopping and starting continued for several minutes, prompting Ana to curiously look forward where she saw streetlight after streetlight turn red as soon as the car pulled up to it.

"I swear," Ana said, "sometimes it's like the whole world doesn't want us to have fun."

After thirty minutes passed, the car pulled up to a curb.

"You get out first," Maria said.

Elena stepped out of the car and was immediately followed by Maria then Ana, who slammed the door shut. As soon as she stepped on the sidewalk, Elena felt her entire body vibrate. She thought it was an earthquake, but when she looked around, she realized the vibration came from the heavy thumping inside the building Maria told her was the club.

Maria was wearing a tight, silver dress that clenched itself around her body. Elena believed she looked far too skinny and was in dire need of a meal. Meanwhile, Ana was wearing a short, tight red skirt and a black shirt that looked more like a cloth with string than any kind of shirt Elena had ever seen. She was also wearing a thick layer of bright red lipstick that contrasted mightily with the pallid white tone of her face. Elena thought she looked sick.

Worried about the health of her friends, Elena was about to voice her concern but changed her mind when after surveying the line-up leading to the front door of the club, she saw that nearly every single girl looked just like them. She believed some of the girls in the line-up, the few healthy-looking ones at least, were pretty underneath all of the powder and make-up. She could not understand why they chose to hide that beauty underneath blotchy white masks.

As she continued to gaze at the girls in the line-up, Elena started focusing on their hair, and just like their bodies, it appeared thin and frail, but what she found the most bizarre was most of them had blond hair, despite having brown eyebrows. She couldn't understand why they would change their hair to a color that looked so unnatural. She could even see the brown roots beneath the golden locks.

When Elena focused on the guys, she noticed many of them exposed even more of their chests than the girls did. She surmised the guys felt the need to expose their chests not just out of some odd aesthetic need, but out of necessity, as it allowed their bodies to breathe, as they, just like their female counterparts, wore obscenely tight and restricting clothing. They also wore glimmering metallic watches far too big for their wrists and had hair that appeared so shiny and greasy that Elena dreaded the thought of touching it.

She didn't understand why everybody in the line-up looked the way they did. Were they embarrassed by how they looked? Were they ashamed? Did they hate themselves that much?

She turned toward Ana, who was also looking at the long line-up of people, but instead of staring and scrutinizing, she was pointing and laughing.

"What's so funny?" Elena said.

"She loves seeing the long lines here," Maria said.

"Why?"

"Because we never have to wait in them."

"We don't?"

"Nope. I'm friends with the bouncer. He always let us in."

Elena walked And and Maria, who made their way right to the front of the line. Steps away from the entrance, Elena looked up and saw a bright red neon sign that read: Perdition.

"Is that the name of the club?"

Ana nodded.

"Why would they name it that?"

"Probably because it sounds cool."

A huge man blocked the three young women from entering the club. His arms were as big as Elena's legs.

Maria stepped forward and playfully slapped the man's bulging left bicep. Ana asked how full the club was. The man, who Elena assumed was the bouncer Maria told her about, said the club was at capacity, and he doubted anybody in the line-up would get in.

Maria leaned toward the bouncer, told him to come close, and she whispered something in his ear. A moment later, with a wide smile, he turned and unclipped the red velvet rope behind him, and with a sweep of his gigantic arm, he allowed Elena, Ana, and Maria to enter Perdition, much to the loud, groaning dismay of those still standing in line, hoping to follow them.

6

Walking through a dimly lit tunnel, Elena could hear the music from within the club thumping louder and louder. She was about to ask Ana and Maria how much further they had to walk, but they had already rushed ahead, throwing their arms up, surrendering to the power of the music.

At the end of the tunnel, Elena absorbed more noise than she had heard in her entire life, but before she could make any sense of it, she was blinded by colorful lights flashing and firing in every direction.

"Isn't this amazing?" Maria said.

Elena couldn't hear Maria's words, the music was too deafening, but she was able to make them out by reading her glossy lips.

All three girls made their way deeper into the madness, toward an enormous bar surrounded by people. Once they got to the bar, Elena grabbed and read a menu. Unsure if she was reading the prices correctly, she double and triple-checked them before realizing they were indeed correct. Nonetheless, she felt obligated to show her new friends appreciation for taking her out, so she reached into her purse and grabbed the cash her mother gave her.

"I want to buy you and Ana a drink," she said to Maria, who was standing beside her.

Maria smiled and shook her head, before motioning for Ana to come close. With her head bowed toward Elena and Maria, Maria told Ana what Elena wished to do. Ana responded by looking at Elena as if she were a child uttering her first word before saying, "Don't worry about it, we were going to buy a bottle and get a table, but that is so sweet of you to offer."

"Are you sure?"

Both Ana and Maria nodded, before Ana said, "Yeah, my dad always gives me enough money to get at least two bottles."

Before Elena could respond, Maria leaned close and looked inside her purse. Not realizing she was still holding the cash, Elena looked up.

"Did you bring all of that just for tonight?" Maria asked.

"My mother saved it up for me so I could afford to live here while I went to school."

"Wait," Maria said, "is that all of the money you have?"
Elena nodded.

"And you think that's going to last you through school?"
Elena said yes.

"That money won't last you a month."

"But my mother has been saving it for ten years."

"Trust me," Maria replied. "If you can hold it all in one hand, it's not enough."

Maria turned toward Ana. Elena didn't have to hear what she was saying to know she was relaying everything Elena had just told her.

Ana turned to Elena.

"You've been carrying all the money you have this whole time?"

"I wanted to keep it with me to make sure it was safe."

"You're lucky."

"Why?"

Ana placed her hand on Elena's shoulder, leaned forward, and said, "That you haven't been robbed."

A waiter appeared in front of the three girls. While balancing a bottle of vodka along with a plastic container filled with ice cubes, a glass jug filled with a blood-red juice and three empty glasses on a tiny black tray, the waiter motioned with his free hand for them to follow him. With the waiter leading the way, the three girls walked until they reached a small table. The waiter placed the bottle, a container of ice, the jug of juice, and the three glasses on the table. He then used a set of metal tongs and grabbed and dropped several ice cubes from the container into each glass and walked away. Neither Ana nor Maria paid him anything, no fee, no tip, no mind.

After the waiter left, Elena asked Ana why she didn't have to pay for what they had just received.

"We're going to get more stuff, so it's easier to just pay the bill at the end of the night."

Elena offered to help with the bill, but Maria just laughed before offering a glance at Elena's purse. Ana told her not to worry about it.

Elena looked around. There were small tables everywhere and each one had at least four people huddled around it, grabbing or holding up bottles. She watched a waiter, whose ability to maneuver his way through was nothing short of amazing, accidentally bump into one of the tables. The table barely moved, and nothing was spilled, but the people surrounding it responded with such scorn that despite the blaring music, Elena was able to hear every word they screamed in the waiter's face. She was both appalled by what the people said and impressed by the waiter's ability to endure it. Afterward, without showing any anger or bitterness, the waiter apologized and walked away before disappearing into the crowd.

Elena turned back toward Ana and Maria, who had already started pouring vodka into the ice-filled glasses. Afterward, Ana poured the juice into each glass. Elena watched attentively as the pure red of the juice was diluted by the alcohol, creating a much duller color. Ana raised her glass high. Maria did the same. Elena followed. Despite the music pummeling her ears, Elena managed to hear Ana say, "Cheers."

Elena's face clenched. Her drink was too strong. In no time, Ana and Maria finished their drinks, while Elena did her best to keep up, finishing hers a few moments later. Immediately after, Ana refilled Elena's glass with ice. Elena was unsure if she should drink any more, but the decision was already made for her when Ana grabbed her glass and refilled it with vodka and just a splash of juice.

Elena took a sip of her drink and realized the more she consumed the less painful drinking it became. In what seemed like no time at all her glass was empty, only to be refilled again.

Two guys approached. They both had the same light skin as Ana and Maria and were dressed in the same tight clothing, with the same hair styles as the men Elena saw in the line-up outside. Without saying a word, one of them grabbed Ana's waist. Elena looked around, trying to find somebody she could call for help, but to Elena's amazement, Ana just smiled. When the guy wrapped his hands around Ana and started kissing her neck while fondling her upper body, she started giggling. Elena turned to Maria and asked if Ana knew the guy. Maria said no. A moment later, the second guy grabbed, kissed, and fondled Maria in the same way.

Elena jumped back after feeling cold liquid strike her leg. She looked at the table. The bottle of vodka had been knocked over. Ana started laughing, while the guy she was with picked the bottle up, while still managing to keep his other arm tightly wrapped around Ana's waist.

Feeling dizzy, Elena tried to tell Maria she needed to go to the washroom, but Maria either couldn't hear her or didn't want to hear her, as she was giving all of her attention to the guy whose mouth refused to release its grip from hers.

With hands constantly touching, grabbing, and rubbing her, Elena felt like she was back on the subway platform. Desperate for space, she rushed to a nearby railing and leaned over it. She saw a pit full of people below, all of whom appeared to be losing their minds. The sight made her tremble. She turned and spotted a waiter. She was about to ask where the washroom was but jumped back after he turned and revealed two bottles on his tray, each one with bright, blinding fireworks exploding from their spouts.

The music suddenly stopped, and the lights throughout the building shut off. The silence was shattered by random screams from people Elena could not see but knew were all around her. She jumped when the sound of a loud horn blared throughout the building. The lights abruptly flashed on, but before she could regain any semblance of calm, a gust of smoke fell upon her and the crowd below. She held her breath, fearful of inhaling, but when she looked around, everybody was reveling in the murky cloud, shouting and dancing within the fog.

Confused as to why people showed no fear at what she thought were the obvious signs of a burgeoning inferno, Elena gasped after hearing an explosion. Not wanting to die in a club filled with people who seemed to enthusiastically welcome being burned alive, she summoned whatever strength she had in hopes of fleeing the building with her life when she heard a second explosion. She looked up and saw an enormous cannon with confetti spilling from its muzzle.

A man's voice screamed from every side, ordering the crowd to throw their hands up, which they did in utter submission. When he turned the music back on and told them to dance, like banshees unleashed they madly moved their bodies, jumping up and down, pounding the floor with so much energy the entire building shook.

Elena recommenced her quest to find the washroom. She made her way through the crowd, fighting for every inch when she finally saw a sign indicating what she had been searching for. She was about to rush inside the washroom but was halted by a long line-up of girls, all waiting to enter. Once it was her turn, she rushed into a stall expecting to vomit immediately, but after several spirited heaves, she was unable to banish what stewed in the pit of her stomach. Elena left the stall, looked in the mirror above the sink, and noticed the lip gloss Maria applied in the car. She brushed her finger against her lips. They felt slimy. Revolted by the feel of the gloss, she turned on the faucet, soaked her hands, and wiped it off until there was not a single trace of it left.

Once Elena was outside of the washroom, she was determined to find Ana and Maria so she could leave Perdition.

She found a staircase and made her way down the steps, barely avoiding a girl in high heels who stumbled and fell to the ground while laughing hysterically. After she scaled the final step, Elena looked forward. She was standing at the edge of the pit, blinded by the lights and pummeled by the music. Even dizzier than before, she tried to kneel, but there was no room. She turned around hoping to make her way back up the staircase, but her path was blocked by a group of girls helping the girl who had just fallen.

Elena started to make her way through the pit of people. After three steps, she could feel the warmth and sweat from the people within. She saw girls rubbing themselves, licking their lips, gyrating against guys who held them tight, fondling them aggressively. She saw girls tilting their heads back as guys poured the contents of bottles into their mouths until several of them began to spit up like babies. She saw girls dancing with other girls, touching each other, kissing each other, while guys surrounded them, staring ravenously.

Now in the center of the pit, Elena felt hands clutching her body. She spun around trying to see who was responsible, but all she could see were blurred figures. She backed up until she struck somebody. She turned. Facing her was a guy with a monstrous smile. He reeked of alcohol. He raised his hands and without saying a word tried to wrap them around her waist. She stepped back. He followed, hands still raised, waiting to swallow her. She looked around, hoping to find a means to escape, but every side was blocked by people dancing. She froze as the guy finally grabbed her and wrapped his hands around her. He rubbed his hands against her lower back. She grabbed his shoulders and tried to push him off, but he refused to release his grip. She tried to speak to him, but whenever she positioned her mouth near either of his ears, he put his mouth in front of hers to kiss her. She wiggled her body, hoping to shake herself loose, but every movement she made seemed to arouse him even more. Finally, after feeling his lips against her neck, she shoved him as hard as she could. Without looking back, she forced her way through the crowd until she made it to the other side of the pit.

Standing before another flight of stairs, Elena looked up, hoping to spot Ana or Maria, but couldn't see either of them. She scaled the steps. Once she reached the top, she breathed heavily. The music seemed louder. The club seemed bigger. The lights seemed brighter. The darkness seemed bleaker. She wanted to sit down, but there were no vacant seats. She felt more hands touching her, aggressively exploring her, violating her, but whenever she looked around, the culprits could never be identified, as they always retreated and blended with the crowd.

She kept moving, believing if she stopped, the club would devour her. She found herself back at the bar, close to the small tables where her journey to the washroom began, but there was no sign of Ana or Maria. Anxious to escape, no longer caring about finding her friends, she tried to find the tunnel she walked through to enter the club but couldn't see it. She leaned against a wall, staring at the floor. She took several breaths. Everything was spinning. She wanted to curl up into a ball. She wanted to cry. She wanted to be back in her bed in her home in her town with her mother.

When she looked back up, to her horror, Elena saw the same guy who grabbed her in the pit. He was so much bigger than her, and as he approached, his eyes wide, his mouth curled into a devilish grin, he grew even larger. For a split second, she wondered if she was just panicking, that maybe he wasn't as threatening as he seemed, but with every step closer, she saw nothing on his face that made her feel comfortable, that didn't make her want to run away. Just before he was within arm's reach a man suddenly stood in front of her. The man turned to her and smiled. It was a genuine smile, a comforting smile, that didn't make her feel like prey. Meanwhile, the guy he had blocked turned and already started making his way toward another girl, who looked to be on the verge of passing out.

"You look like you need some air," the man said before extending his hand, which Elena took.

He guided her through Perdition, effortlessly moving those who stood in front of him out of the way while making sure the only hand touching her was his.

After spotting the tunnel she knew would finally lead her out of the club, Elena squeezed the man's hand tighter. He led her through the tunnel, guiding her powerfully, but not forcefully. Every step provided more relief, as every step diminished the relentless pounding of the music.

When they finally reached the end of the tunnel, she closed her eyes after feeling a gust of wind brush against her face. She breathed deep, taking in as much air as she could.

When she opened her eyes, she saw the man standing in front of her. He was tall, but not intimidating. He was handsome but didn't look as if he tried very hard. He looked simple in the best possible way.

"My name's Diego."

He looked like a prince and the way he stared at her made her feel like a princess.

7

A hand grabbed the back of Elena's shoulder. The grip was weak, and the hand was small. When she turned around, she saw Ana's pale face. Maria was standing beside her. Both girls smiled while staring at Diego.

"Who's this?" Ana said.

Diego introduced himself.

Ana couldn't stop smiling at him.

Elena was about to ask what happened to them inside of the club and was about to tell them about the ordeal she endured trying to find them before Diego rescued her. But before she could say a single word, Maria told her they were going home because they had drunk too much and wanted to pass out.

"Do you need a ride back?" Maria asked.

"But she lives so far," Ana said, "and we're just a few minutes away. I feel like shit. I want to go home now."

Elena stayed quiet, worried about what she was going to do when Diego intervened.

"I can drive her back."

Ana pulled out her cell phone and made a brief call.

In what seemed like no time at all a car pulled up to the curb, the same car that picked Elena up from the city square and took her, Ana, and Maria to the club.

"Have fun the rest of the night," Ana said before disappearing into the car's backseat.

Before following her friend into the vehicle, Maria handed Elena a piece of paper.

"It's my phone number. Give me a call, so we can hang out again."

After the vehicle drove away, Elena turned toward Diego, who was staring at her.

"You're beautiful," he said.

Unsure how she was supposed to respond to such direct compliments, Elena replied with a sheepish thank you.

"So where am I taking you?"

She told him she was staying at a hostel near the city's main square, not far from the cathedral. She was anxious to hear Diego's response, curious if he would have an expression of disgust like Ana and Maria did, but to her surprise and delight, he did the opposite and nodded his head approvingly.

"I think the square is one of the most interesting parts of the city. It's one of the biggest in the world, you know? A lot has happened there over the years. A lot of history was made."

Elena was anxious to hear more, to learn about what happened, to discover that history, but before she could ask, he pointed down the street, saying his car was parked nearby.

The walk was slow, and Elena enjoyed the leisurely pace. It allowed her to listen to Diego talk about what it was like growing up in one of the city's northern sections.

"We didn't have much, but that motivated me to work hard, so I could get out of there."

"You grew up poor?"

"I don't like to think too much about it. It was a long time ago."

She wondered about the ambition he had to possess or had possibly possessed him, to escape poverty he would not tell her about. So she imagined it instead, envisioning him overcoming obstacle after obstacle on his way to a victory so complete that he was able to casually dismiss it.

Elena moved closer to him, brushing her body against his. He stopped, looked down, smiled, leaned in, and kissed her. She closed her eyes. It felt strange but incredible. She didn't have much experience. She hoped she was doing it right. She wondered if he would have liked it better if she left on the lip gloss. When the kiss was over and she opened her eyes, she desired nothing more than to kiss him again. He appeared to have different plans, however, as he turned, raised his arm, and pointed at a silver car that shimmered despite the darkness trying to stifle it.

She took several steps toward the spotless vehicle before stopping and standing in front of the passenger's side door. She leaned toward the window and looked inside. The interior was flawless. Every seat was covered with black leather. While she had seen cars of similar style before, she never had the opportunity to look at them for more than a second, as they were always speeding down the highway that cut through her hometown.

"Do you like it?"

"It's beautiful."

Diego opened the passenger side door, and with a sweep of his arm, he allowed her to get inside the car, just as the bouncer allowed her, Ana, and Maria to enter Perdition after unclipping the red velvet rope.

Elena couldn't believe how comfortable, how soft the leather seats were, and when she thought back to the metal slab she sat on inside the subway earlier in the day the seat in Diego's car felt even better.

After closing the door, Diego walked around the car, opened the driver's side door, and slid into his seat. He offered Elena a bottle of water that she immediately started drinking.

"Thank you so much for rescuing me in the club," she said.

He looked at her with an expression of what appeared to be anger, which made her nervous that she said something wrong.

"I've seen guys like that more times than I can count. I've known guys like that growing up, too, so when I saw you I knew I had to do something."

She smiled with relief.

"I'm glad you did," she said. "It was scary in there, so many people grabbing at me. It felt like they were trying to tear me apart."

Diego shook his head.

"I'm so sorry you had to go through that. I hate how women have to suffer that kind of abuse whenever they go out. It's wrong and it's disgusting. We need to do more to protect them."

Diego drove through the city's streets, passing cars with ease and zooming through intersections with confidence. They chatted, though it was mostly her answering questions about herself. He asked about her background, and why she looked the way she did. She told him both of her parents came from families with deep roots in the south of the country. He asked about her hometown and her upbringing. She gave a brief, vague description of the simple life she and her mother had forged together after her father died almost ten years earlier. He asked why she left and came to the city. She told him about her acceptance to the university.

Throughout the conversation, Elena gazed at Diego, marveling at his concentration as he stared through the windshield at everything in front of him. She gazed at his strong hands as they flexed while gripping the steering wheel. She blushed whenever he glanced at her.

The car pulled up in front of the cathedral where Elena's evening began. Diego turned off the ignition.

"How far is your hostel from here?"

She told him it was very close, well within walking distance. She told him she didn't want to inconvenience him and would be okay to get there on her own.

"This square, while interesting during the day, isn't that safe at night. How long are you staying at the hostel?"

"I'm not sure. I don't start school for a month, and I decided to stay there for a couple of nights until I got more familiar with the city and then maybe find somewhere else."

Diego appeared to be contemplating something, but whatever it was he kept to himself, as he replied with a nod and a charming grin before restarting the car, insisting he would drop her off directly in front of her hostel.

When the car pulled up in front of the hostel, Elena was unsure what to say or do. She grabbed the door handle, hoping Diego would say something, hoping he would grab her shoulder and ask her to wait, to stop. When she heard the door click, scared to look back, she pushed the door open. With one foot on the curb, she could feel the firm concrete against the bottom of her sandal. She took a deep breath, turned her body, and put her second foot on the ground. After another breath, she moved her entire body but stopped when she felt Diego's strong hand grip her shoulder, just as she hoped it would.

She turned around and stared at him. He looked perfect.

"Did you want to get together tomorrow, maybe get something to eat, walk around? I can tell you about the city, and help you get acquainted with it."

She emphatically said yes.

"How about I come to pick you up tomorrow, at two o'clock?"

Elena nodded, knowing she would have said yes regardless of what time he said.

"Do you see that bench over there?" he said, pointing at a bench near the giant flag hanging limp against the massive flagpole.

Elena turned and put both of her feet back into the car. She leaned toward Diego, looking to where he was pointing, and said she could see the bench.

Diego turned toward her. She remained exactly where she was. He leaned toward her. She kept still. He pressed his lips against hers. She wished they would never let go. When they finally did, he said, "I'll see you tomorrow, right, two o'clock?"

She leaned back toward Diego, extended her hand, and pointed at the national flag and the bench resting near it, before kissing his cheek.

"I'll see you there."

"You are so beautiful," he whispered. "I can't believe I found you."

He rested his hand on her thigh. His grip was strong, but not restricting. He squeezed her skin. She felt her entire body shiver. She put her hand on top of his. She took two deep breaths before attempting to lean in and kiss him again, but he removed his hand, and to her horror leaned back and said, "You should get some sleep."

Vanquishing her terror, he followed his words with a smile that was every bit as comforting as the hug he followed it up with.

Feeling his arms wrapped around her body, Elena felt safe and secure in a way she had never felt before.

"Have a good night, Elena."

Elena twisted her body around, opened the door, and got out of the car. She closed the door, gently, doing everything she could to prevent it from slamming, before turning, kneeling, and looking through the window at Diego. He smiled back at her, and with her eyes wide open she fantasized about him.

8

⚯

Refreshed after a long sleep that took hold of her as soon as her head hit the lumpy pillow, Elena put on another one of the dresses her mother made for her. It was colorful and vibrant, wavy and free. It was the dress her mother had spent the most time making, and the one Elena cherished above the rest. She hoped Diego would like it.

Standing in front of the cracked mirror hanging on the wall near her bed, she brushed her hair and teeth, put on her sandals, and left the room. She checked her watch. It was one-twenty. She didn't want to be late, not by a minute, not even by a second.

The square was full of people, but all she could see was the bench. She walked toward it. When she was within a few steps of it, she noticed a woman making her way toward it. She quickened her pace and got to the bench first. She sat in the center and placed her purse beside her, making it abundantly clear nobody except for Diego was welcome to sit with her.

The bench was uncomfortable. Wooden splinters poked her thighs. She moved her body, shifting it constantly, trying to find a position tolerable enough to sit until two o'clock.

She swayed her feet while doing her best to avoid the splinters. She took long, deep breaths. She checked her watch incessantly.

With only five minutes to go, her thighs stinging from the splinters and aching from the constant swaying, she stared at the perpetually moving crowd. She believed she had seen Diego's perfect face attached to at least five different men.

She looked down at her watch. It was exactly two o'clock. She looked up, expecting to see Diego standing over her, smiling, offering his hand, which she envisioned grabbing, feeling his strong, powerful grip, before allowing it to raise her from the bench, but there was no sign of him.

The moment her watch read one minute past two o'clock, she started to panic. She rubbed her palms together, and traces of perspiration moved from one hand to the other. After five more minutes, she once again looked at the faces in the crowd, believing they were all staring back at her, laughing. At a quarter past the hour, she wanted to get up, walk away and find a quiet place to cry, but in a city where people seemed to occupy every available space, she doubted such a place existed. Another fifteen minutes passed. With her hands now pressed against the bench, her exhausted, ravaged thighs tensed with anticipation. She made sure nobody was in front of her, obstructing what she hoped to be a swift, clean getaway. She closed her eyes and took one last breath before she was ready to rise and walk away from the bench, but when she opened her eyes, there was Diego.

"I'm so sorry for being late, but traffic here, no matter how early you leave, how much you plan, always has the final say as to when you arrive."

Elena wanted to dismiss him and walk off, but when she stood, willing, ready to do so, he grabbed her hand, and before she knew it, with his hand securely clasped around hers, they walked away from the bench. Once they reached his car, he opened the door for her, and she got inside. The blaring noise of the city quieted to a whisper.

Diego effortlessly made his way through the never-ending traffic.

There was a red streetlight ahead. Diego slowed the car before it came to a stop. Elena saw a small boy standing before the long line of anxiously waiting vehicles. The boy, who was so filthy she was unable to tell if his skin was as dark as hers, or as fair as Diego's, wore clothing so tattered it appeared moments away from falling off his body. In the boy's hands were two batons, both on fire, and a small black stick. The boy spun the batons with the stick before tossing them in the air and catching them while narrowly missing setting his hair on fire. After the terrifying show was over, the boy casually put out the flames and walked toward the line-up of cars. He tapped on Diego's window. Without even looking down, Diego reached into a small compartment below the car's dash-board, grabbed a few coins, pushed a button that lowered his window, and handed them to the boy. The boy silently accepted the money before immediately moving down the line to the next car. The boy moved quickly, trying to reach as many cars as he could before the streetlight turned green, and all of the cars, with Diego's vehicle leading the way, drove through the intersection.

"I knew a lot of kids who had to do that growing up," he said, "and I always told myself I would never let that happen to me."

Elena gazed at him, admiring his ability to rise from the position from which he was born, hoping she could do the same.

"I thought we could get something to eat. After that, I wanted to take you to some of the best parts of the city, the nicest, safest parts, not too far from where I live."

"That sounds perfect," she said.

When Diego pulled up to the curb of Elena's hostel, nightfall had already taken hold of the city. She looked at her watch and couldn't believe how late it was.

Before exiting the car, Diego asked her if she wanted to see him again the next day. She immediately said she did before leaning toward him and kissing him.

The following day, she waited on the same bench she did the day before, but there was no tension, no stress, no doubt. She knew she would see him and could not wait to do so.

When he finally arrived, Diego sat next to her. He reached into his pocket and held out a balled fist.

"What's that?"

He smiled and opened his hand. Resting in the center of his large palm was a silver smartphone.

"It's for you, a gift."

She grabbed the phone. It was almost weightless and was already turned on. She had seen smartphones before, but never ones this sleek and fancy looking. She used them a few times, too, but never owned one.

"Go to contacts."

Elena followed Diego's instructions and saw only one name listed.

"Now you can get a hold of me whenever you want."

"Thank you so much," she replied, marveling at the decadence of the device.

"I have something else for you."

After reaching into his other pocket, he pulled out a small watch. Its metallic band had a bright silver sheen, while the dial had an elegant, glacial blue background with shiny Roman numerals marking every hour. Elena, nervous to even touch the timepiece, did not accept it at first, but after glancing at Diego, who responded with an encouraging nod, her apprehension vanished.

"It's beautiful. I love it."

She extended her arm, ready to accept the gift, but paused after noticing the plastic watch her mother gave her years ago wrapped around her wrist. She looked at the watch's dial. It had a picture of a character from one of her favorite childhood shows in the center that never failed to make her smile, while the watch's band, despite being made of cheap rubber, proved remarkably steadfast, surviving for years.

Diego grabbed her wrist, unclipped, and deftly removed the old watch before swiftly replacing it with the new one. A patch of Elena's skin was momentarily caught in the metallic watch's clasp after Diego clipped it together, causing a quick burst of discomfort that was immediately forgotten.

"Do you still want this?" Diego asked, holding up the watch her mother gave her with the tips of his thumb and forefinger.

Elena looked down at the new gift tightly wrapped around her wrist, and with her attention fixated on the gleaming watch dial, she said no.

9

Elena had seen Diego every single day that week, and every day the week after. Every time he saw her, he took her somewhere new, showed her something new, taught her something new, and bought her something new, from a new black leather purse to a pair of oversized sunglasses, all while constantly telling her how beautiful she was. However, the one gift that stood out most of all came on the fifth day of that week, when as soon as she got into the car, he held up a small paper plate covered in tin foil.

"What's that?"

"Open it."

She didn't have to. She could already smell what she couldn't believe rested underneath the glimmering shroud.

"It can't be."

He smiled.

"I guess you'll have to find out."

She accepted the plate, removed the tinfoil, and gasped. The only thing that hit her harder than the surprise was how something she so undeniably loved, yet wanted to desperately escape from, could smell so good and bring back so much.

"You remembered?"

"How could I forget?"

"But how were you able to find it here? I thought they only made it in this style in my hometown?"

"I told you, Elena, you can have everything you miss right here, in the city, with me."

She was overwhelmed with uncertainty as to what she appreciated more, Diego listening to her description of her favorite dish (after her mother's *tinga*, of course), right down to the absence of onions, to the genuine pleasure she could see on his face for doing something that made her happy.

After dropping Elena off at her hostel following yet another one of their long, shared days together, Diego got out of the car, stood, and stared at the building. Elena curiously watched him before asking if something was wrong.

"You've been staying here for a week now, right?

"Yes."

"Do you like it?"

"It's okay."

Diego turned and asked her how she was going to keep paying to stay there once school started.

Elena didn't answer. She knew even though Diego had been paying for everything while they were together, the collection of cash her mother gave her had nonetheless reduced in size to the point where she had to use another, smaller rubber band to contain it. She realized Maria was right, that the money her mother spent over a decade saving would probably not last a month in the city, but she did not want to tell Diego that. She did not want to burden him, even though she was worrying more and more about what she was going to do when the final sliver of cash was gone.

"I know how expensive this city is, Elena."

Elena looked down at the ground. Overwhelmed with shame, she could not look up and could not muster a response. Unsure what to expect from Diego, she just stared at the cracked pavement.

"I know a way you can save whatever money you have left and a way we can see each other even more than we already do."

Elena looked up and said, "How?"

"Move in with me, in my condo."

For the first time since she met him Elena could see anxiety in Diego's face as he awaited her response.

"When would you want me to move in?"

"Why not right now?"

Elena felt like she did when caught between the two colliding waves of people at the entrance of the subway train. While she was unsure if moving in with Diego was the right thing to do, she was afraid if she took too much time thinking about it, she would offend him, and he would break off whatever it was they had together. So, just like she did with the subway train, she allowed momentum to push her forward.

"Okay," she replied. "Let me go back to my room and get my suitcase."

"I'll help you," he said.

Diego and Elena walked up to the reception desk, where a young woman Elena didn't recognize was busy typing on a computer. Elena said she was going to be checking out.

The receptionist did not look up from her computer screen and said, "Okay."

After they reached Elena's room, she pulled out her shabby suitcase from the narrow closet and packed the few items she possessed.

"All done," she said with a smile.

Diego took several steps back until he was standing in the hallway and said, "Now let's get you to a nicer place."

The drive to Diego's condo did not take long, yet despite the short distance the difference between the chaos of the city's main square and the serenity of Diego's neighborhood was astounding. They passed park after park, each one clean and green, the exercise equipment inside sleek and shiny. Every park was full of children, watched mostly by older women wearing purple and red aprons that Elena immediately recognized, as her mother owned several of them over the years. Meanwhile, the streets were calm, with people casually walking up and down the clean, level sidewalks, smiling and chatting. There was no pushing, no shoving, no tired eyes, and no desperate faces. No squalid children were tossing flaming batons into the air at the intersections, and nobody was curled on the ground, begging for change.

"How far are we from the university?" she asked.

"It's pretty far, but I wouldn't worry about that right now."

"I just hope it's easier to get there by subway from here than it was from the square."

"Do you like taking the subway?"

"I'm learning more every time I use it."

"I know, but do you *like* taking it?"

In truth, Elena hated taking the subway, dreading it every single time she entered a station. Just the thought of the smells, the sweat, the unwanted eyes glaring at her and the aggressive hands touching her made her shudder. She still had a hard time resisting the urge to panic and scream whenever a car filled to the brim with people, suffocating her, and the train abruptly stopped midway through a tunnel for what felt like years. But she didn't want to tell Diego all of that. She also didn't want to lie to him, so she softened the truth by replying, "Not really, but it's not that bad."

"I know how bad it is," he replied, "especially for women. I've seen how men harass them all the time, touching them and bothering them, and for a beautiful woman like you, it must be even worse."

"It can be uncomfortable sometimes, but it's just part of living in the city, right?"

"Wouldn't you prefer to get around the city in this car?"

The decision was obvious, and he had to know that, but she didn't want to seem too eager to accept, as the last thing she wanted him to think was that she was using him.

"Are you sure?" she asked.

"Of course. I won't take the subway, so why should you?"

"I don't go a lot of places. I will mainly just be going to school once it starts."

When Diego's car pulled into the garage underneath what Elena assumed was the building where he lived, he made several quick turns before pulling into a parking space. After she stepped out of the car, all she could see were spotless, fancy cars. Almost all of them resembled Diego's, right down to the silver hood ornaments. After Diego opened the trunk and took out Elena's suitcase, they boarded an elevator and rode it to the eighth floor. Elena was terrified. She had never ridden in an elevator before. But she kept her fear to herself, not wishing to bother Diego. When the elevator stopped, she stepped out and took several deep breaths, before following Diego to the front door of his condo. After he unlocked the door, turned the handle, and pushed it forward, he walked inside and took a step aside, allowing her to enter.

She walked into the condo but jumped after hearing a clap of thunder that sounded too close to be real. Diego apologized and said, "It's a heavy door, so it makes a loud slam whenever you close it. It's a small price to pay for security."

Elena collected herself and said, "It's no problem."

"So," Diego replied, still holding Elena's suitcase in his hand, "what do you think?"

"I think it's beautiful. I have never seen a place like this before. The floors, the furniture, the walls, everything looks so perfect."

"I work hard, so I can get things like this, things I want to share with you, Elena."

There it was again, she thought, his hard work, his ambition to be more than he was born to be.

"Thank you so much, Diego."

She looked around Diego's home again and started tapping her foot, just to get a sense of how solid it all was, how real.

"I know this might sound weird, Diego, and I hope you won't laugh at me, but ever since we met you've made me feel like a princess."

Diego placed the suitcase on the floor and approached her. When he reached her, he placed both of his powerful hands on her shoulders and gripped them tightly.

"You are a princess."

Elena smiled warmly.

"Thank you for not laughing at me."

"I love you, Elena."

Taken aback, trapped in his powerful embrace, staring at his eager eyes, she felt compelled to respond immediately.

"I love you, too."

Diego released his hands from her shoulders, stepped back, and said, "This is your home now."

She looked around again, this time for much longer than she did before. Never in her wildest dreams did she believe she would ever be able to call a place as impressive as Diego's condo home.

She turned back to where Diego had been standing, anxious to express her appreciation once again, but he was no longer there. Her suitcase was gone, too.

"Diego?"

There was no answer. Elena repeated his name, but there was still no response. She walked further into the condo, venturing into the living room, where she stared in amazement at the television set propped against the wall. She refused to get too close to it, fearful it would fall and crash to the floor if she so much as breathed on it.

After three steps, she was obstructed by a leather-bound sofa. She called out Diego's name again, but there was still no reply. She sat. The cushions exhaled deeply as she leaned back and sank into them. It felt as soothing as it sounded.

After a few minutes, Elena rose from the sofa and made her way into the kitchen. It was enormous and full of appliances, most of which she had never seen before. Everything was neatly organized. The counter was spotless. The floors were pristine. The refrigerator was huge, but she was weary of opening it, not wishing to be disrespectful. She gazed at the dining table, imagining herself and Diego eating a meal she had prepared.

She walked down the condo's main hallway. It was long and wide, sharing the same spaciousness as the living room and kitchen. What she found odd, however, was the absence of photographs. There was not a single picture of Diego, or his family, about whom he had barely spoken about since they met. There was nothing but a vacant, white wall, a canvas of an absent past.

Midway down the hallway, she saw a door. She opened it and walked in. From the sink to the tub to the toilet to the floor itself, the entire room was immaculately white. Elena took a nervous step toward the sink. She wanted to wash her hands and face but was hesitant to touch the glistening silver faucets, afraid to smudge them with her fingerprints. So she grabbed a towel hanging from a rack, wiped her hands and face, and placed the towel back on the rack, carefully positioning it so it looked like it had not been moved.

Back in the hallway, Elena turned and walked to the end. Standing in between a pair of closed doors, each one directly across from the other, she chose the door on the right and walked in. After turning on the light, she saw a large desk, covered with papers neatly stacked in spots she did not dare disturb. There was a black, leather-bound swivel chair resting in front of the desk, three high rising cabinets placed side by side by side, and a large bookcase filled with books and sealed boxes. Recalling their second date when Diego told her he worked from home, where he managed exporting accounts for different clients, Elena realized she was inside his office. She was in awe at how organized, how professional, how prestigious it appeared. It was where his ambitions came to life.

After backing out of the room slowly, making sure she did not accidentally bump into anything, she turned off the light and closed the door. She opened the door on the opposite side.

The light was already on. A huge bed rested in the center of the room. Never had she seen a bed so big. It was covered in a thick comforter, with six plush pillows neatly positioned together. She couldn't help but think about her old bed in her childhood home. She remembered the meager mattress, the single sheet, the quilt her mother made for her, and the single lumpy pillow.

With her eyes still focused on the bed right in front of her, she yearned to feel the softness of the comforter, to rest her head on every single one of its plush pillows, to roll from one side of the vast mattress to the other.

"Welcome to the master bedroom."

She saw Diego standing inside the closet. He was lifting her suitcase above his head until he was finally able to put it on a shelf that she would never be able to reach on her own.

After his hands were free, he reached into his pocket, pulled out his closed fist, and walked toward her. Staring at his knuckles, Elena stood motionless. With a wide smile on his face, Diego looked directly at his fist. He slowly rotated his wrist until his knuckles pointed to the floor. He opened his hand. Resting in the center of his palm was a small red velvet box. He opened the box with his other hand, revealing a diamond ring.

"Will you marry me?"

Tearing her attention away from the large, sparkling diamond fastened atop the silver-colored ring, she looked up at Diego. His smile had disappeared, replaced by an expression of concern.

"You just asked me to move in with you a few hours ago, now you want me to marry you?"

With the distress on his face intensifying, making her regret what she said, Diego replied, "Of course, why else would I want you to move in with me if I didn't also want you to be my wife?"

"What about school?"

"Why exactly do you want to go to school, Elena?"

"It's been my dream for as long as I can remember."

"But why is it your dream?"

"Because I want to make a better life for myself. I want to be more than I was born to be, just like you, Diego."

"Thank you for saying that, Elena, but I didn't even finish high school, so ambition has nothing to do with getting a degree, it's about doing what needs to be done. I'm sure you've explored this place already. You've seen how nice it is. I can give you that. I want to give you that. All you have to do is say yes."

Elena turned away from him to think clearly, but all she could see was the beautiful bed and the enormous window draped with the most lavish curtains she had ever seen.

She looked back at him and said, "But I've always wanted to go to university, Diego, and I'm going to start classes in just a few weeks. How can I focus on my classes, while also getting ready to get married? How can I study when I'm also learning to be a wife?"

"Remember when you told me about the first time you saw your faculty building and how you ran toward it, and how you couldn't wait to walk inside, but it was locked?"

She nodded.

"Did the building look like it was run down like it was falling apart?"

She said no.

"So, it's safe to say the building will be around a year from now, probably many years from now, right?"

"I guess so," she replied.

"So why not wait a year?" he asked. "Why not go to school next fall instead of this one?"

"But I got accepted for this year, and if I want to attend school next year, I'd have to do the entrance exam again, and it was hard, Diego. I had to study for months."

"I think you're the most amazing woman I've ever met, Elena. I have no doubt you could pass the entrance exam again."

She didn't reply.

"Most people want to go to school so they can get a good job and create a better life, the one you dreamt of creating, right?"

She said yes.

"I already have a good job, Elena. I've already done the hard work. I've already created the better life you would've had to spend years building from scratch. Ambition only matters if you get the desired results, and those results are already here for you. All you have to do is say yes, and you'll get the life you've always wanted, and you won't have to wait for four or eight, or ten years to get it. You'll have it right now."

Diego pushed the opened red velvet box even closer to her face. The diamond appeared even bigger and brighter than before.

"I know this is sudden," he said. "I know we've only known each other for a short time, but what does time matter when you know what's right?"

She saw tension on Diego's face, and it got more intense with every passing second. It was clear her silence was torturing him. For him to want to marry her after such a short time, he must have seen more in her than she had ever seen in herself.

"Yes, Diego, I'll marry you."

All of the tension in Diego's face disappeared in an instant. Relieved, Elena grabbed the box with the ring inside.

"I promise I will take care of you, Elena. I promise I will protect you and I promise I will love you, for the rest of your life."

Elena carefully grabbed the engagement ring and removed it from the box.

"It's beautiful," she said. "I love it."

"Let me help you put it on."

Elena handed the ring to Diego. He gently positioned it around her finger and pushed. The ring rose smoothly up her finger until it reached her knuckle. It wouldn't move any further. He grabbed her wrist with his free hand, using it as leverage, and forced the ring past her knuckle. Elena winced and looked down. The ring was too tight, and the dark skin of her finger, below and above where the ring now rested, had turned white.

10

⁓

A perfectly sized wedding ring slid up Elena's finger smoothly until it collided with the engagement ring just above her knuckle.

Diego took a step back while gazing at his new wife.

"You were a princess," he said. "Now you're a queen."

After leaving the chamber where a judge legitimized the union, the newly married couple went out to dinner before Diego drove them back to the condo. During the drive, Elena told her new husband that she wanted to visit her mother, to tell her the news in person.

"Of course," he replied. "I promise we'll go when the time is right."

When they reached the condo, Elena walked to the bedroom. She opened the curtains. The evening had taken hold. Through the enormous window, she stared at the city lights, focusing on the ones covering the mountains warmly embracing the sprawling metropolis. She stared at them reverently, while remembering the vast, terrifying darkness on the other side.

She turned after hearing Diego's steps approaching from behind.

"What are you looking at?" he asked.

"The lights over there, on the mountains."

She raised her hand and pointed at them.

"No matter how many times I see them, I can't stop thinking how bright and beautiful they are, like stars you can touch."

Diego laughed then wrapped his arms around her body and squeezed. She could feel his breath against the back of her neck. She closed her eyes, smiled, and tilted her head back, nestling it against his chest.

"What's so funny?" she said.

"Don't you know what those lights are?"

She said no.

"They're from a bunch of neighborhoods called the Devil's horns."

"Why are they called that?"

"I honestly can't remember," he replied, "but those neighborhoods are some of the poorest, most dangerous areas in the city."

Diego broke the embrace and took a step back. Elena turned around and faced him.

"The lights are still nice to look at though, just don't get too close to them."

She smiled.

"Diego," she said.

"Yes."

"I can't believe I'm married."

"I can," he replied.

"Wait, Diego, what day is it?"

"Monday, the fourth."

Elena shook her head.

"What is it?" he asked.

"Today would have been my first day of classes."

"One year from today can be your first day of classes."

Elena thought about the campus and the faculty building she stood in front of less than a month ago.

Diego walked to the bed and sat.

"I know you wanted to wait until our wedding night to be intimate, Elena, and you know how much I respected that decision. I never complained. I never pushed."

"I know, Diego, and thank you for that."

"Tonight's our wedding night."

Elena remained where she was.

Diego rose from the bed, approached his wife, and wrapped his arms around her. He kissed her on the cheek, then on the forehead, before kissing her on the nose and the lips. With his hands still wrapped around her body, he started moving them up and down. His touch was enticing and scintillating. He squeezed her tighter. She marveled at his strength. Her breathing slowed. Her eyes closed. She felt as if she were no longer standing, but floating. Diego tilted his head down and whispered, "I want you."

His breath warmed her earlobe.

"I want you, too, but I haven't done it before. Can we take it slow? Can we kiss more first?"

"Of course."

Every kiss made her yearn for the next one, and the one after that. She rubbed his arms, strong and firm, and with her eyes closed, she got lost in the warmth, the comfort, the safety of his lips, and his embrace. She had lost count of how many soft kisses they had shared, but when the last one didn't immediately lead to another, she opened her eyes and saw Diego take a few steps back while removing his shirt. She stared at his upper body, gazing at his muscles, each one appearing to ripple independently of the other.

Elena took several steps forward before stopping just short of touching him. She wanted him even more than she did just a few minutes ago but enjoyed the playful anxiety of imagining touching his body and imagining kissing his mouth, feeling the caress of his soft lips.

He stepped toward her, smiled, and gripped the corners of her dress, and in a single motion, he swept those corners off her shoulders. Despite her underwear still covering her most private parts, Elena frantically moved her hands to cover herself up even more. So immersed in how much she wanted him, she was caught off guard by his action, and was nervous at how suddenly uncomfortable she felt, how exposed.

"Why are you covering yourself?" he asked. "You're beautiful."

"I'm sorry, Diego, and thank you because whenever you say it, I always believe it, but this is the first time for me. I'm just nervous. Can we just keep kissing? I like that. I like it a lot. It feels really good. Doesn't it feel good for you, too?"

"You are so beautiful, Elena. From the first moment I saw you, I thought you were the most beautiful woman in the world. Your skin, your breasts, your arms, your hips, your legs, oh Elena, your eyes, your lips, your hair. And that is just your body, but you, as a person, as a woman, are incredible. Your bravery to come to the city alone, your ambition to be more. I am the luckiest man in the world to be here, with you, right now."

Still standing in her fallen dress, Elena was overcome with pride at her new husband's words, and while she wanted to give him everything he wanted from her and more, she nonetheless hoped that he would accommodate her request to keep kissing, to keep feeling good, to keep feeling comfortable. She looked down at the dress her mother made for her laying in a crumpled heap. When she looked back up, Diego was no longer just shirtless, he had also taken off his pants. Wearing nothing but his underwear, he gestured for her to come to him.

She remained where she was. She glared at his nearly naked body with eager anticipation, to touch it, hold it, kiss it and enjoy it, but when she stared at what remained covered, her nervousness returned.

"Diego. I want you. I do. You are so handsome, so strong, and I can't wait to spend the rest of my life sharing pleasure with you, but for tonight, can we please just keep kissing, holding each other, and touching each other. I would like that because when we take things further, something I want to do, I want to be completely comfortable, and as into it as you are. Wouldn't that be better?"

Diego approached her, wrapped his arms around her, and slowly spun her while keeping her within his embrace.

He kissed the back of her neck. He rubbed her chest. She started to moan. He turned her back around. All she could see was him. He leaned forward and kissed her. Her entire body felt like it was plugged into him, and she could feel his energy, his power. Feeling his hands exploring her body while his lips continuously massaged hers was heavenly. Pleasure had never existed to her as it did at that moment.

Diego abruptly broke the passionate embrace, turned around, and made his way toward the bed, but stopped just short of it. He turned back around, raised his hand, which Elena dutifully took, and pulled her to the bed until she lay on the soft sheets covering the enormous mattress. They continued kissing, their hands exploring their bodies, their shared moans growing more intense.

He turned the lights off. She couldn't see anything but was not afraid because he continued kissing her. It wasn't until he suddenly stopped kissing her that she started feeling uncomfortable, awkward, in the dark, not able to feel her husband's lips or a gentle touch. She felt relief when his hands started caressing her face. She then felt his lips pressing against her cheek, and a rush of warmth and pleasure alleviated the temporary bout of discomfort. He then started kissing her neck, before progressing further down, touching parts of her body he had never touched before. The nervousness returned, despite how good his touch felt.

He removed her bra. She instinctively tried to cover her breasts with her hands, but Diego used his larger, stronger hands to ward hers off. She felt those very same hands caressing her bare breasts, massaging them. It felt good, but the nervousness only grew. A moment later, after feeling his hands moving further down, softly exploring her stomach, he took off her underwear. The nervousness had intensified even more. It was confusing how even though what he was doing felt so good, the closer he got to her most intimate parts the more distant he felt from her, and her from him. She desperately wanted to rewind things, to get him back to where he was, to have his lips pressed against hers, to feel his hands touching the parts of her body she had just gotten comfortable with.

"Are you ready?" he asked.

Unable to see him, only able to hear him and feel him, she wasn't sure what she was supposed to be ready for. Her ignorance made way for panic. For a while, there was room for only pleasure and joy, but things had shifted, and she started feeling that whatever control she had was gone, that whatever sense of comfort she enjoyed had disappeared.

The girth of Diego's body pressed on top of her, taking her breath away. There was a sudden rush of pain. Her eyes burst open, but she could only see darkness. She didn't know what was happening. She didn't understand why it was happening. Most of all, she wanted it to stop happening.

"It hurts, Diego," she whispered. "Can we please stop? I just want to do what we were doing before. I just want to kiss you, and I just want you to kiss me."

"I love you," he said.

"Diego, it hurts."

"I love you."

"Diego, please."

"I love you."

Realizing her words were being ignored, she no longer spoke and dismissed the notion of asking him for help, since he was the one inflicting the pain. With every thrust, she bit her lip as hard as she could; her only relief came in not being able to feel her teeth because, during those excruciating moments, she didn't even feel as if she was in her own body.

After Diego's final thrust and the feeling of something rushing inside of her, he rolled off of her, allowing her to breathe, deep and free. Naked and exposed, she was drenched in sweat, both hers and his. She felt drained and overheated as if she had just stepped foot on the sweltering subway platform after forcing her way through the crowd. And just like the subway, she felt the same sense of powerlessness, suffocation, and confusion.

Still staring at nothing but darkness, hoping the next time will feel better, she felt the softness of Diego's lips pressed against her left ankle. Unable to see him, she nonetheless tilted her head forward, knowing her husband was there, at her feet, kissing her ankle for reasons she could not understand. When he was finished, he repositioned his body until he was lying beside her and said, "I love you so much, Elena."

11

After lifting the comforter she had covered herself with as she slept, Elena sat up but stopped when she glanced at her left ankle and noticed something metallic wrapped around it. It was spotless and emitted no sound. It wasn't very large or thick, and when she raised her leg, she barely noticed any additional weight. While securely fastened, it wasn't tight and caused no pain. She leaned forward, but just before the metallic object was within her grasp, she froze after hearing Diego say, "You shouldn't tamper with it."

She looked up and saw Diego standing in the doorway, a towel wrapped around his waist. His powerful upper body glistened as drops of water rolled down his chest and arms.

"What are you talking about, Diego? What is this thing?"

He calmly wiped away some of the water from his face and hair.

"I put it on your ankle while you were sleeping."

"Can you please take it off?"

"I can't."

"What do you mean you can't?"

"We're married now, and it's my job to be with you, all the time, and to keep you safe, all the time. All you have to do is stay within one hundred meters of me and you'll have nothing to worry about."

Elena started shuffling her body in the bed to make sure she wasn't dreaming. She felt afraid when she realized she wasn't.

"I don't want this piece of metal wrapped around my ankle, Diego."

"Is the device uncomfortable? It's supposed to be sized perfectly."

Whether or not it's comfortable doesn't matter. I don't want it there at all."

"I told you, Elena, I can't take it off."

She leaned forward. She knew she was awake, that it wasn't a dream, but she needed to touch whatever was encircling her ankle. She needed to know it was real, but just before her outstretched fingers made contact, Diego approached, smiled warmly, and said everything was fine.

"Diego, what is going on?"

"You just have to stay within one hundred meters of me. That's all. It's a long distance. You won't even notice."

Her hands started perspiring so much that she had to wipe them on the bed.

"What happens if I'm more than one hundred meters away from you?"

"The device will explode."

Elena felt her whole body go numb. She started to breathe rapidly but calmed herself before a smile crept across her face.

"Very funny, Diego. For a second, I believed you. I did. I even started getting scared, like really scared. You got me. You got me."

He stared back at her.

"Okay Diego, seriously, it was a great joke, but you can take this thing off now."

"It's my job to protect you, Elena, and I need you by my side all the time so I can do that."

Refusing to believe the unbelievable, Elena forced a feeble laugh before raising her left leg and pointing at the device clamped around her ankle.

"How is this protecting me?"

Diego sat on the bed next to his wife and replied, "It keeps you close to me, so nothing can happen to you, ever."

His face looked like a soldier's gun, and that's when Elena realized he meant every word. She leaned back and rested her head on the pillow. Diego lay beside her and ran his fingers through her hair. She could feel the warmth from his freshly showered body.

"I just want to keep you safe, Elena, and how can I do that if I'm constantly worrying about you? How can I do that if I'm always wondering where you are, who you're with, who is following you, or who is thinking about you? Where I grew up, I saw how terribly men treated women, and nothing was ever done about it, it just kept happening, and it's most likely still happening, but with that device I can protect you from those kinds of men by always keeping you close to me."

With her eyes locked on her husband's, Elena desperately tried to find a lack of conviction that would reassure her nothing she saw and nothing she heard was true.

"Don't you remember when you talked about how you felt on the subway after you got off the train, how you felt hands touching you and grabbing you, and how awful it felt, and how aggressive it was? Or what about the club where we met when you said you felt like those men inside were trying to tear you apart and how scared you felt? Now, you'll never have to worry about feeling that way ever again."

Diego kissed Elena on the cheek, told her he loved her, got off the bed, and told her he was going to get changed. Refusing to believe what was happening, she lunged forward and wrapped her fingers around his wrist, hoping the sudden clench would somehow break the spell from which he seemed to be held captive. He turned around.

"So, what happens if I decide to call the police and tell them what you did?"

He shook his head. She could feel his contempt.

"I can't believe you'd make a threat like that, Elena, when all I'm doing is guaranteeing your safety for the rest of your life."

She threw her hands up, trying to physically exercise the absurdity of the situation.

"How is putting a bomb on my ankle guaranteeing my safety?"

"I'm not just giving you safety, Elena. That device also represents my promise to give you the best life possible. Do you remember when you told me about that Indian woman and her kids you saw on the subway, begging for money, and how sad it made you feel?"

Elena nodded.

"This device ensures that you will never have to worry about ending up like that woman, and when we have children, they will never end up like those kids you saw. That's how much I love you, Elena."

She shook her head and replied, "What if we get a divorce?"

"Marriage is forever, Elena."

"What happens if I decide to leave you in the middle of the night, while you're sleeping?"

"Once you're more than one hundred meters away from me, the device will explode."

Elena buried her face in her hands, but refused to cry, knowing that if she did there was no coming back from that; if a single tear was shed that meant it was too real to escape.

"And how will I even know when I'm close to one-hundred meters away from you?"

"The device will start to loudly beep once you reach a certain point, and it will keep beeping louder and louder until you reach one-hundred meters."

"You'd kill your wife?" she asked, doing all she could to mask her fear at the potential answer.

"I would never hurt you, Elena. I love you, and that's why I'm explaining to you why I put the device there, to make sure you're always taken care of, to make sure you're always protected, always safe."

She didn't reply. She couldn't reply.

Diego got up from the bed and approached the closet. As he started picking out the clothes he was going to wear for the day, Elena closed her eyes in a bid to escape what had to be a nightmare. But, when she opened her eyes and looked down, all she could see was the device wrapped around her ankle, looking and feeling as real as the bed she was laying on.

"You should have a shower and get dressed," Diego said. "We're going to the mall."

Elena didn't reply. Her attention was still focused on the device.

"Oh, and don't wear one of your mom's dresses."

She turned away from the device and looked up at Diego. "What?" she said.

"You'd be better off wearing pants."

"But I don't have any pants, Diego. I just have the dresses my mom made for me. You know that."

"Sorry, I forgot to tell you, but I bought a pair of jeans for you, and some socks and shoes, too. I've been meaning to tell you that you shouldn't be wearing sandals in the city either."

"But I like my sandals. That's all I wore in my hometown."

Diego pointed at the drawer where he said the pants, socks, and shoes were, and said, "This isn't your hometown."

He made his way toward the door, but stopped, turned, and walked back toward Elena, who had covered her entire body up to her face with the comforter. He leaned down when he reached her. She hoped he would remove the comforter first and the device second, before telling her it was all a joke. Instead, he softly kissed her on the forehead before turning back around and leaving the room.

Elena kicked her left foot from underneath the comforter until the device was visible. She stared at it, consumed with fear at the thought of touching it. After a deep breath, she sat up and twisted her body around, accidentally bumping the device on one of the bed's wooden legs. She held her breath, but nothing happened.

She went to the washroom and took a shower. She watched drop after drop of water splash against the device, but its shimmering hide held firm. After she got out of the shower, she dried herself, put on her underwear, and walked back into the bedroom, staring at her ankle the entire time.

Elena opened the drawer where Diego said her new pants, socks, and shoes were. She pulled a pair of white socks out and tossed them on the bed. She pulled out the pair of jeans. She knew immediately they were too small. She tried to stretch them, but the denim was unforgivably stiff. She tossed them on the bed. She opened a small shoe box. She looked at the shoes. They were a pair of bland grey sneakers. She didn't like them and just like the jeans, she was certain they were too small. She put the shoes back in the box and tossed them on the bed.

She grabbed the jeans and even though she knew they wouldn't fit, she still tried putting them on. When she managed to get the waistband past her hips, she took a breath and instantly regretted exhaling when the jeans' button pinched her stomach. She inhaled, adjusted the button, and exhaled cautiously until she was convinced no pain would result from the laborious task of breathing. The unrelenting denim clasped itself around her hips and thighs but loosened just enough around the ankles to prevent her from seeing the device.

She grabbed the socks and bent down to put them on but unleashed a yelp as the jeans' button pushed into her like a dull knife. She sat on the bed, took a deep breath, sucking in her stomach as much as she could, held it, leaned forward, and pulled the socks on as fast as she could. Afterward, she repeated the same process so she could put on the shoes, and just as she thought, they were too small and crushed her feet just like the jeans crushed her hips and thighs.

She stood and slowly, painfully walked back toward Diego's drawer, realizing she didn't have any shirts either. She sifted through several of his shirts and found a simple, plain grey t-shirt. She put the shirt on, and while it was too big for her, she welcomed the size difference because unlike the shoes and jeans it didn't strangle her body.

Diego walked in, looked his wife up and down, laughed, and said, "Is that one of my shirts?"

Elena nodded and said she did not have any shirts either.

"Sorry," he said. "I must have forgotten to get some for you. We'll get you some shirts today, too."

"Diego, can you not see the jeans don't fit? I can barely breathe, and the shoes are too small."

"No problem," he said. "We'll buy you some new jeans, new shoes, some new shirts, and whatever else you want, Elena."

"I don't like wearing jeans, or shoes, or t-shirts, or even socks, Diego. I like wearing the dresses I came here with. I like how they look. I like how the material feels on my skin when I wear them. It's the same with my sandals on my feet."

"This city is filthy, Elena, and if you keep wearing sandals, you'll end up getting sick."

"And why can't I wear my dresses?" she asked. "If it's about the device and people seeing it, Diego, then just take it off. I want it off."

"I told I can't take it off, Elena, and you can't keep wearing the dresses because you look too beautiful in them, and they show too much of that beauty," Diego said. "Trust me, it's for the best."

She would have preferred if he had just told her he didn't want her to wear the dresses because he didn't want people to see the bomb clamped around her ankle. At least that reason would have made sense to her, but to be told she couldn't wear her favorite dresses because she looked too beautiful in them was ridiculous.

"Why didn't you tell me all of this before we got married? You didn't have a problem with my dresses or my sandals before, so why now?"

"I wasn't your husband then, so it wasn't my place to say what you could and couldn't wear, but I'm your husband now."

"But Diego--"

"I love you so much, Elena, but I don't want to argue about this anymore. I'm going to the car, and I suggest you follow me."

12

⁓

The parking lot in front of the enormous building Diego casually referred to as the mall was packed with cars, but he still managed to find a space. As a result of the wrong sized jeans and shoes, every step Elena took toward the palatial structure hurt.

When they finally reached the mall's entrance, Elena froze after seeing two men in police uniforms standing in front of the doors, cradling machine guns. She looked at Diego, who didn't seem to notice the gun-toting men as he walked right past them. Elena focused on the guns themselves and spotted several dents and chips in the almond-colored stocks and patches of rust on the barrels. When she looked up at the faces of the men wielding the weapons, she saw nothing but boredom, making them appear far less threatening than the soldiers she had seen routinely throughout her life.

Diego walked through the building's massive glass doors. Elena followed him inside. She shivered when hit with a wave of cold air and was blinded by the bright lights shining from every direction.

"Don't forget to stay close to me," Diego said.

Elena followed Diego as he proceeded down a vast corridor, avoiding the thralls of people with the same ease he used to navigate through the city's oppressive traffic. She was not as successful, however, bumping into so many people she started to question if they were aiming for her. She said sorry so many times after a while she was convinced the word was meaningless, as those who seemed to hear her never responded, and those who did didn't seem to care.

Due to her inability to make her way through the human traffic, Elena started lagging behind Diego. She estimated the distance between them to be somewhere between ten and fifteen meters. While it was a far cry from one hundred, just having to calculate the distance between her and her husband was infuriating while knowing all of her efforts were the result of nothing but Diego's word, made her even angrier. She felt herself gaining more courage by the second to stop and scream at him, telling him he had lost his mind before walking away from him forever, device and its beeping be damned. But, after yet another person bumped into her, the question of how many innocent people would share her fate if there was any truth to her husband's words entered her mind. When she looked to her right and saw a man and woman walking, each one of them holding the hand of a small, smiling child, she felt sick to her stomach. When she returned her attention to Diego and noticed the distance between them had grown even more, she panicked. And even though she knew she was still well within one-hundred meters of him, and she didn't hear any beeping from the device, she nonetheless ran toward him, shoving aside anybody who got in her way until she caught up to him.

While forcing herself to keep up with Diego's long strides, Elena started looking around. All she could see was store after store and the spotless panes of glass protecting the elaborately set up displays of the products they sold inside. She glared at the faces of the mall's consumers, particularly the girls. She felt as if she were back inside Perdition, as she immediately noticed the same fake blond hair and bleached, made-up faces, along with the same short skirts and tight shirts. She focused on the girls' ankles, trying to spot a device, and when she could not see any traces of one, she wondered if they had devices placed on one of the few parts of their body she could not see.

Diego quickened his pace, forcing Elena to speed up even more. The pain in her waist, legs, and feet grew more intense. He changed direction before making his way toward a gigantic store that appeared to be the crown jewel of the mall. He turned around, and said, "This is Buckingham."

As soon as she stepped foot inside of the store, Elena was overwhelmed by the powerful stench of various perfumes. The scents were so powerful they burned her nose and made her eyes water.

She tried to follow her husband's lead through the endless rows of booths, but they seemed to be set up for the sole purpose of obstructing her. She bumped into one of them, prompting the attention of the representative sitting behind it. Staring at Diego, panicking as he got further away from her, she immediately tried to get back on course, but the female representative stood in her way and refused to let her pass.

"Please, I have to go, my husband is over there. I have to catch up to him."

"Don't worry. He'll be fine. You should try this."

The representative raised a small bottle and told Elena to raise her wrist. Before she could refuse the perfume, the representative leaned forward and sprayed some of it on Elena's wrist. Elena couldn't help but inhale the scent. It was lovely. The representative started to pull out more bottles from a drawer in her booth, saying the exotic name of each one with infectious enthusiasm. Elena looked around, trying to spot Diego. When she finally saw him, to her horror, she immediately realized the distance between them had already doubled and was on the verge of tripling.

Elena said she had to go, but the representative was insistent and pulled out different lip sticks, eye shadows, and powders.

"I can see you don't wear much make-up," she said, "you're very pretty, but if you used some of these things, along with that perfume, you'd be even pret--"

"I'm sorry," Elena interrupted, "but I have to go, my husband is getting far away, and I have to stay close to him or bad things will happen."

The representative raised her hand, flashing an engagement ring with a diamond much smaller than Elena's.

"Trust me, I know how it is."

Elena glanced at the representative's ankles, curious if there was a device clamped around one of them, but they were covered by the cuffs of her pants.

The woman stepped aside, allowing Elena to pass.

After Elena walked by, she paused, turned back, and looked at the representative, still wondering if she had a device attached to her body. The representative did not look back at her, however, as she had already found another young woman to tempt with the abundance of beauty products at her disposal. After turning back around, Elena dashed through the maze of booths and representatives, until she finally reached Diego, who was standing in front of an elevator, waiting for the doors to open.

"Where were you?"

Elena had to catch her breath before replying, "I was held up. I'm sorry."

"It's okay," he said, before turning toward the elevator doors that had just opened. "Come on."

Elena followed him into the elevator. Staring through the windows, she watched as everything beneath her grew smaller the higher up they went.

"Are you okay?"

Able to see the full scope of the labyrinth of booths below, she gasped at how many people there were, many of whom she had not even seen. There must have been hundreds of them, and all of them would have been killed or maimed by the blast if the device had exploded.

"I'm fine."

She couldn't understand why Diego didn't seem the least bit worried when she finally caught up to him. He had to be aware of how far away from him she was. It had to be at least thirty, maybe even forty meters, a gap she thought was large enough to warrant at least an expression of concern.

The elevator doors opened. Diego stepped out first. Elena followed. Diego looked up, read a large sign dictating what was where, and started walking straight ahead. Elena followed.

The married couple was soon surrounded by racks of women's clothing and lifeless mannequins. Elena approached one of the plastic statues. There were no eyes to see, no mouth to speak, no ears to hear. It had lily-white skin, and a slim, yet voluptuous figure, looking nothing like her, or the vast majority of other women she saw in the mall, despite their best efforts.

She glanced at Diego, who was sitting on a nearby bench.

"Pick whatever you want and don't worry about the price. If you like it, get it."

Elena grabbed a pair of jeans dangling from a hanger just beneath a mannequin wearing a similar-looking pair. The mannequin looked perfect in the jeans since it had no hips to speak of.

"Try them on," he said.

Elena looked around, confused as to where she was supposed to try on the jeans. Diego directed her toward a row of change rooms. She entered one of the cramped rooms that had nothing inside except for a long mirror hanging on the wall and took off her shoes and her jeans. Her feet and hips exhaled with relief. Basking in the painlessness, she looked down and the first thing she saw was the glimmering device wrapped around her ankle. She tried on the jeans. They were far more forgiving than the pair Diego got her.

It took a few more minutes for Elena to pick out more pairs of jeans, along with the shirts and shoes Diego said she needed. None of them appealed to her. The shoes, while comfortable, lacked the vibrant color of her sandals, while the shirts and jeans lacked the richness of her dresses, but Diego said he liked them, so Elena let him get them for her.

13

Rain and hail terrorized the city, falling on the heads of everybody beneath it, from mothers tightly gripping their children's hands, doing all they could to keep them safe, to businessmen in fine suits and expensive shoes tiptoeing their way around massive puddles on the sidewalks and roads.

Sitting at a small table with two vacant chairs across from her, Elena watched the storm's fury from inside a fancy cafe near Diego's condo. The cafe was filling up with people. Some were trying to dry themselves by shaking their bodies like dogs, while others rubbed their heads, trying to relieve themselves of the pain they suffered after being struck by one of the storm's crystallized pellets.

She looked up and saw Ana and Maria. They appeared untouched by the downpour. She stood, anxious to welcome them and curious to know how they managed to avoid getting soaked by the rain or struck by the hail, but before she could say anything, Ana said, "You've lost so much weight."

"It's true," Maria said. "You look great."

Elena sat back down. Ana and Maria sat in the two vacant chairs across from her.

Elena apologized for not contacting them earlier, and was about to explain why, when Ana shouted, "Oh my God, you got married!"

Elena looked down, saw her hand on the table, and realized Ana had spotted the two rings wrapped around her finger.

"They're beautiful," Maria said, "so is that new watch, and your new purse, too."

"Look at the size of that diamond," Ana said. "It's huge."

"Who is the lucky guy?" Maria asked.

"Diego," Elena replied, "the guy from Perdition."

"Wow, that was fast," Maria said.

"Good for you," Ana said. "Any guy willing to buy a ring with a diamond that big is worth locking up."

With Ana and Maria's eyes still fixated on the rings wrapped around her finger, Elena thought about the device wrapped around her ankle. She debated how she was going to bring the device up, hoping they would help her get it removed.

"How long has it been since we saw each other?" she asked.

"A couple of months," Maria replied.

Ana pulled her phone out of her purse and laughed at whatever it was she saw on the screen before placing it on the table.

"Let's get back to your weight loss," she said. "How were you able to lose so much weight in so little time, Elena? What's your secret?"

"I'm still getting used to the food Diego likes. It's a lot different than what my mother used to make, so I'm eating less than I did before."

Ana nodded in approval.

"And what about your skin, it looks fairer."

She thrust her arm forward and placed it on the table beside Elena's.

"It's almost as light as mine," she said.

She started running her finger against Elena's arm as if she were attempting to see if the lighter shade was phony and could be removed like a streak of dust.

"How did you do it?"

"I haven't been going outside much," Elena replied after pulling her arm away, "and the few times I do there's no sun. There has barely been any sun since I got here.

Maria, who had been typing on her phone throughout Ana and Elena's exchange, put her phone on the table, well within her reach, looked at Elena, smiled, and said, "So, what have you been doing now that you're married?"

Elena didn't answer immediately, as she was fixated on Maria and Ana's phones. They were nice looking, with the same sleek, stylish shape as the one Diego gave her, but she couldn't help noticing the minor scratches, of which her phone had none.

"Nothing much," Elena finally replied. "I mostly just clean the condo, cook, and help Diego with his work. He works at home. He's very busy, so I try to help whenever I can."

"I bet he is," Ana said. "He has to be working a lot to be buying diamonds like that."

"I also watch TV," Elena said, "which I'm starting to like."

"You're talking as if you never watched TV before," Maria said with a laugh.

"I didn't," Elena replied. "My mom and I never had one."

Both Ana and Maria glared at Elena with confusion before looking at each other and laughing.

"So, how is school?" Elena asked, anxious to change the subject, while still hoping to eventually steer it toward the device wrapped around her ankle.

"It's school," Maria said. "It's exactly like high school was, just with more people, harder work, and a crappier building. I guess now we know why you haven't gone."

"I still plan on going," Elena said. "We just decided it was best to wait a year."

Elena crossed her legs, then uncrossed them before crossing them again. She was unsure why. It could have been boredom, or it could have been hoping that either Ana or Maria would notice the device so she could finally talk about it.

"Why bother?" Ana said. "You already found a husband, and you didn't even have to spend a single day in university to do it."

"Tell us more about married life," Maria asked.

Hoping that was her cue to steer the conversation where she wanted, Elena glanced down at her ankle, ready to reveal the device, but just as she opened her mouth, just as the revelatory words rose, a waitress arrived holding three menus. She was about to place the menus on the table when Ana asked Elena and Maria if they wanted coffee. Elena nodded. Maria said yes.

"We'll just have coffee," Ana said.

The waitress nodded and walked off.

Frustrated by the interruption, but still resolute, Elena once again summoned the words she believed would help her get the device removed.

"After the wedding night--"

Cutting her off, Ana said, "Oh my God, how was the wedding night? How was he in bed? I bet he knows what he's doing."

Maria giggled.

Discouraged, Elena didn't bother acknowledging the question and tried to continue, but was once again thwarted when Maria said, "Wait, isn't that him over there, sitting at that table?"

Ana looked around for a few moments, before pointing toward where Elena already knew Diego was sitting.

"That's him," Ana said. "I remember his face."

"He likes to stay close to me," Elena replied, noticing Ana's smile.

"That's the sweetest thing ever," Ana said, "and for him to sit so far away just to give you your privacy. That's amazing."

"It's true," Maria added. "All of the guys I've been with always had to be right beside me, all the time, even when I was with my friends. You're lucky, Elena. He gives you space."

Ana and Maria stared at Diego just like they stared at the diamond perched atop Elena's engagement ring. Elena leaned forward, about to whisper to them about the device, but with people continuing to pour into the cafe in an attempt to escape the storm outside, the noise level had reached a point where it would have been impossible for them to hear her, so she pulled herself back and sat straight. Confident it was loud enough inside the cafe for her to speak in a normal tone of voice without Diego being able to hear her, she said, "There is something I want to tell you, something I'm not sure you'll believe."

Maria returned her attention to Elena, while Ana continued staring at Diego. Elena didn't like how intensely Ana was staring at her husband, and how big her smile was while doing it, but it did at least let her know exactly where he was.

"What is it?" Maria said.

Elena took a deep breath and said, "I don't know how to say it. I'm confused. I'm not sure exactly what is happening, and I hate to say it, I hate to even think it, but I'm scared."

Ana's attention shifted back toward Maria and Elena before she leaned close to them in an attempt to be part of the conversation.

"Why?" Maria said. "What's wrong? Does he hit you?"

"No, nothing like that."

"Does he cheat on you?"

"He would never do that."

"Does he yell at you? Does he insult you?"

"No, and anytime he does yell, he always apologizes right after."

"Does he ignore you?"

"That's the last thing he'd do."

"Is he taking care of you?"

"He takes care of everything."

"Does he make sure you're safe?"

"He's obsessed with my safety."

"Does he love you?"

"He loves me more than I thought a person could ever love somebody else."

Ana stared at Elena contemptuously before saying, "So what the hell is the problem? You barely had any money. You lived in a crappy part of the city, and he rescued you. He gave you a better life. He doesn't hit you. He doesn't cheat on you. He keeps you safe and he loves you. If you didn't marry Diego, you'd probably end up like that waitress over there, serving people coffee, while having to go to school, and that's if you were even able to find a job at all. You should be telling us how amazing it is to be married to a man like that, and how thankful and appreciative you are to have found him. You said it yourself that you didn't even have a TV where you came from, so I don't know why you're whining about how confused and scared you are. You have no idea how lucky you are."

Before Elena could say anything, the waitress arrived, holding a tray with three small cups of coffee balanced on top of it.

No longer wondering how she was going to expose the device, Elena started debating if she should expose it. She wondered if they were right and she was seeing things completely wrong, and instead of doubting, fearing, and complaining, she should have been feeling grateful and lucky for having a husband like Diego. She started wondering if the device was just a small price to pay for the amazing life he had given her, and the love he had shown her, even if that small price would explode if she ever broke its only rule.

Elena felt a hand grip her shoulder. She turned around and saw Diego standing over her. He was looking at Ana and Maria.

"Hello," he said.

Both Ana and Maria smiled, said hello, and before Elena could say anything, Ana asked him if wanted to sit down. To make sure he was heard over the noise inside the cafe, Diego shouted at the people sitting at the nearest table if he could borrow one of their vacant chairs. They said yes. He lifted the chair and placed it right beside Elena with a loud slam.

The waitress returned and asked Diego if he wanted anything. He said no. After the waitress left, before any conversation could start, Diego said he and Elena had to leave. He turned, saw the waitress, and mimicked signing a bill. A moment later she returned with the check, which Diego insisted on paying. Both Ana and Maria thanked him, and in the case of Ana a little too aggressively for Elena's liking. After Diego stood, Elena got up, followed by Ana and Maria. After exchanging goodbyes and embraces, Diego walked toward the door. Elena started following her husband but was stopped when she felt a hand grab her wrist, preventing her from taking another step. Before she looked back to see who grabbed her, she stared at Diego, watching him rapidly increase the distance between them. She watched him reach the door, looking as if he was going to open it and pass through the doorway at any moment. She looked at the bustling crowd inside the cafe. There were even more people than when she first arrived. She spun around, anxious to know who was preventing her from joining her husband and putting so many innocent lives at risk. She saw Maria. As soon as Maria saw Elena's face, she immediately released her grip.

"I just wanted to tell you he's amazing, Elena, and you're so lucky to have him."

Elena turned around and looked back at Diego, who had already passed through the doorway. Horrified when the door closed behind him, Elena didn't respond. She dashed through the cafe, nearly tripping halfway, before reaching the door. Barely breaking stride, she pushed the door open, ran through the doorway, and to her relief saw Diego standing outside.

"I'm sorry," she said, "Maria just wanted to tell me something."

Diego smiled, kissed her on the cheek, took off his jacket, and held it up and over his wife to shield her from the falling rain and hail before guiding her to his car.

14

―――――――― ❧ ――――――――

"Is it far?" Elena asked.

"No," Diego said.

Elena looked through the car window. The sun was shining. She pushed a button. The window lowered, allowing her to not just see, but feel the sun's rays on her skin.

"Put the window back up," Diego said. "You know how much I hate having to breathe the exhaust fumes from the other cars.

Elena pushed the same button. The window rose back up. Diego pressed a button on the car's dashboard. Cold air started blowing out of a vent.

"If you're hot, just let me know, so I can turn on the air conditioning."

She rubbed her arms.

Diego pulled the car into a large parking lot where he found a spot, parked, turned off the ignition, and stepped out. Elena remained inside. She pulled up the cuff of her jeans and stared at the device clamped around her ankle. The device looked every bit as perfect as it did the morning it was put on her. After letting the cuff of her pants fall back down, she smiled, envisioning what it was going to be like after finally having the device removed. She wondered if her ankle would be itchy, or if it would have a rash. She wondered if her ankle would be covered in dried sweat, or if there would be a dreadful patch of unruly, dark hair.

She hoped Diego would not get in trouble for what he did. She believed he was a great man and a great husband, who despite how misguided his actions did what he did because of the overwhelming love he felt for her, but he had to know the device could not be kept around her ankle forever and it was going to get removed at some point. She just hoped he would not be angry when it finally happened.

Stepping out of the car, Elena stood wide-eyed when she saw the building in front of her. It looked like a temple built with bricks of pure white light. Once she walked in, her mouth gaped open.

"This is a hospital?"

Diego didn't answer. He was too busy reading a large sign listing where every department was located, from the maternity ward where they brought life to the world to the morgue where they threw death away.

"What?" he said.

"This is a hospital?" Elena repeated, even though she was already certain of the answer.

"This way," he replied, ignoring the question yet again.

Elena followed her husband to an elevator and watched him push the button. While they waited, she asked him why the building looked the way it did.

"It's a private hospital."

"How can a hospital be private?" she said, looking around at the lavish spaciousness of the building.

Diego didn't answer. The elevator arrived. They both stepped in. The walls of the elevator were built with spotless glass. After the doors closed, the elevator made its way up, allowing Elena to gaze through the windows just as she did in the elevator inside Buckingham. She saw beautiful sculptures and paintings in every corner of the ground floor.

After the elevator stopped, Diego stepped out first. Elena followed. They walked into a quiet, pristine waiting room. Elena sat on one of the many vacant chairs. Looking around, she was amazed that in a city overflowing with people a room with more vacant chairs than occupied ones could exist.

After briefly speaking with the receptionist, Diego sat on the chair beside Elena and said, "The doctor will see us in a few minutes."

Elena shook her head.

"What is it? Are you okay?"

"I'm fine," she replied. "It's just, this hospital, it's so crazy to see."

Diego leaned back in his chair and looked at his wife as if she were a child, proud despite their ignorance, before responding, "What's so crazy about it? Haven't you been in a hospital before?"

"No."

"How is that possible?"

"There wasn't one near our town, and if anybody ever got sick, they had to find a way to get the nearest doctor's office, and that was two hours away."

Diego shook his head, placed his hand on Elena's shoulder, squeezed it, and said, "That's awful, but you don't have to worry about that anymore. This hospital is where people like us are supposed to go."

She didn't respond.

"What happened to those people in your town who were sick, but couldn't make the trip to the doctor's office?"

Now it was Elena's turn to look at Diego as if he were the proudly ignorant child, before replying, "They either got better, or they died."

The receptionist looked up from her desk. "The doctor will see you, now. Just through there."

Before walking through the door, Elena paused and glanced at her ankle and the device concealed by her jeans. If the device could hear her words, she would have happily told it to enjoy the next few minutes, as they would be its last.

"Hello Mr. and Mrs. Escobedo, my name is Doctor Roberto Trujillo. It's a pleasure to meet you both. So, you think you're pregnant?"

Elena was about to respond but held her words back after realizing the doctor was only addressing Diego.

"Yes," Diego replied. "My wife did a test yesterday and it said positive, so we came here to confirm it."

The doctor, whose eyes never left Diego's, smiled and said, "We'll perform some tests and get you that confirmation in no time."

Diego turned his attention to Elena, the first time since entering the office either of the two men looked at her.

"Are you ready for your exam?" he said.

Before replying with the yes she had been rehearsing in her mind ever since Diego told her where they were going, Elena unleashed a smile wider than the one she had after receiving her university acceptance letter months earlier.

"Excellent," the doctor said.

"Mr. Escobedo," he said, "would you like to join us in the examination room?"

Elena looked at her husband, unsure how he was going to answer, unsure if he wanted to see the device being removed. To her surprise, however, without any sign of reluctance, he said yes.

Led by her husband, following the doctor, Elena was guided into a room that on any other occasion would have frightened her. Cold to the point where her skin started to harden, the interrogatingly bright, white, sterile room felt like a place where joy was forbidden to enter. Nonetheless, she still had the same wide smile she walked in with.

"Mr. Escobedo, we're going to proceed with a physical examination before the blood test."

Elena was ecstatic. Her smile grew even wider.

"Mrs. Escobedo," I'm going to need you to go into that washroom right over there, take off your clothes, and put on this gown."

The doctor handed Elena a gown. It felt like a clump of thin tissue paper, just like the kind she used to use back in her hometown.

"Should I take off everything?" she asked, all the while knowing she was going to do so anyway, regardless of what the doctor said. She wanted to make sure he saw the device clamped around her ankle.

"Yes," he replied.

She wanted to bring up the device to her husband. She wanted to ask him how he felt about it finally coming off. And though he did not confirm the device's removal at any point before coming to the hospital, she assumed it was a foregone conclusion when considering the possibility of pregnancy. She believed there was no way Diego would leave it on if she were carrying his child.

With her smile still firmly intact, Elena walked into the washroom. After turning on the light and closing the door behind her, she took a deep breath, placed the gown on the floor beside her, and started to undress. She removed her shirt, pants, underwear, socks, and shoes. She grabbed the gown, but not before lifting her left leg and gazing at the device. Its grey, metallic sheen appeared just as clean, just as shimmering, just as perfect as ever. Unlike past occasions, however, there was no apprehension, no fear, no awe when she saw the device, only a spiteful desire to hear it crack and snap. She wanted to see it broken, thrown out, and destroyed. While she would not have been surprised if there was a method to remove the device without it having to endure a single scratch, she hoped that method would not be utilized just so she could see it suffer.

Still reveling in the thought of the device's torture and demise, Elena grabbed the gown and put it on. Once she managed to manipulate the flimsy material until it finally resembled an article of clothing, she glanced at a small mirror. She stepped back and saw as much of herself as she could. She noticed the pale hue of her skin but knew once the device was removed, she would insist on going outside all the time, even when Diego was working, while wearing the dresses she loved, exposing the skin she yearned to replenish with the sun it had been denied. She noticed her weight loss but knew once the device was removed, she would seek out restaurants that served the type of food she loved, alone, so she could replenish her dissipated figure. She would restore herself to the person she was, and in a few months, she would take the university entrance exam again, pass and finally start school.

She turned around, grabbed the door handle, took a breath, took one last glance at the exposed device, turned the handle, and opened the door. She walked out with a long stride, followed by another and another, each one showing the device in all its glory until she was in the center of the room. She did not know what to expect, what kind of facial expression the doctor would have, what he would say, or what he would do. What if the doctor assaulted Diego for what he had done? What if he called the police and had Diego arrested? How long would her husband have to serve in jail for putting a bomb on her ankle as she slept?

She wished she had put more thought into how she was going to expose the device, but it was too late. She had already crossed the point of no return. She closed her eyes and waited for whatever was to come.

"Mrs. Escobedo, if you could please sit on the bed over there."

Elena opened her eyes and saw the doctor staring at her, smiling.

She approached the bed as requested, but instead of the long confident strides she took when exiting the washroom, she walked in short, hesitant steps. Once she reached the bed, in another effort to make sure the doctor noticed the device she couldn't believe he didn't yet comment on, she bumped it against the bed's base. There was a loud clanging sound. She stared directly at the doctor, but he made no reaction as if he didn't hear the noise at all. She looked at her husband, who didn't appear to hear the noise either. She hopped onto the mattress. It was hard and stiff.

"Could you please lie down," the doctor said.

Elena did as she was told. Flat on her back, she tilted her head and stared at the device staring right back at her, shining triumphantly as it reflected the white light permeating the room.

The doctor started asking Elena questions, but she barely heard them, paying as much attention to them as the doctor was paying to the device clamped around her ankle. She couldn't believe he didn't see it. It was right in front of his face, yet he acted as if it wasn't even there, making her question if it was even there.

While staring at the ceiling, unsure what was real and what was not, Elena followed the doctor's orders as he proceeded to examine her. She glanced at Diego. His attention was focused entirely on her.

When the physical exam was over, the doctor told her to sit up. He told her he was going to take some blood. He walked to one of the room's many metal cabinets, opened it, and pulled out a capped syringe, tourniquet, and three small, empty vials. He told her to hold out her arm.

"Which one?" she asked.

"It doesn't matter," he replied.

Still trying to figure out why what she wanted to happen wasn't happening, Elena was unable to even make the simple decision as to which arm to volunteer, so she looked at Diego, who said, "Left."

She did as she was told. With her left arm held up and extended, she watched the doctor tightly wrap the tourniquet around her upper arm. Her fingers felt numb. She felt a rush of cold as the doctor rubbed a small patch of skin on her forearm with a wet cotton ball. He removed the cap from the syringe, revealing the needle.

"This might hurt a little."

Diego grabbed her other hand, squeezed it, and said everything would be all right. But, instead of looking back at her husband, she stared at the needle and watched it come closer to her skin before it touched and then punctured it. She didn't make a sound, while feeling momentarily soothed by the pain of the needle's entry.

"Are you okay?" Diego asked.

She didn't answer. She just watched her blood fill up the first vial, followed by the second and the third.

The doctor turned his attention to Diego and said, "I'm going to drop these off, and we should have the results in less than an hour."

"Thank you," Diego said.

"It's my pleasure," the doctor replied. "Your wife can put her clothes back on, and if you can take a seat in the waiting room my secretary will let you know when the results are ready."

Diego nodded, while Elena remained on the bed, staring up at the white light emanating from the ceiling. She felt pressure on her hand. She turned and saw Diego holding it while leaning against the bed, a big smile on his face.

Elena shook her hand free of her husband's grasp, got off the bed, and walked back into the washroom. Once inside, after closing the door behind her, she tore off the gown and put back on her underwear, socks, shirt, and jeans, the latter concealing the device. She lowered her head, knowing the device was celebrating its victory and was doing so in the most humiliating way possible, by staying silent and letting the victory speak for itself.

After putting on her shoes, Elena didn't bother offering the mirror a glance because there was nothing she wished to see. She approached the door, turned the handle, walked out, and allowed herself to be encased by her husband's awaiting embrace.

"I can't believe it," he said. "I don't even need the confirmation to know what I already know. We're going to have a baby, Elena. We're going to be so happy. Everything will change. I promise."

Elena glanced down at her concealed ankle.

Led by Diego, they walked out of the examination room and made their way to the waiting room. There were so many vacant chairs to choose from it took them a few seconds to decide which ones to occupy.

Time moved slowly. Elena constantly stared at the beautiful watch wrapped around her wrist, while Diego fidgeted and stared at the floor. Nearly an hour had elapsed before she saw Dr. Trujillo walk through the door. He was smiling. She knew. Diego looked up, saw what she saw, and with his hand gripped tightly around hers he jumped out of his seat, forcing her to jump with him.

Diego rushed to the doctor, taking Elena with him, pulling her arm so powerfully she felt a faint pop in her shoulder. Once they reached the desk where the doctor was leaning, he smiled at Diego and nodded, never once looking at Elena. Diego let out a shout of pure joy.

"I'd like to see Elena in a few weeks," the doctor said. "It's still very early. It looks like she's only at six weeks right now, but I'd like to keep a close eye on things."

"Of course, whatever needs to be done," Diego said.

After future appointments were scheduled and good-byes were exchanged, Elena and Diego left the waiting room, took the elevator back down to the hospital's ground floor, walked out of the building, and approached the car. No words were spoken. Diego maintained a dreamy grin the whole time. It was a smile, a state of being, that Elena didn't wish to break.

After Diego opened the passenger side door for her, Elena sat in her seat, grabbed the seatbelt, and was about to pull it across her body, when Diego grabbed it and did it for her, tugging at the belt several times, making sure it was as tight and securely fastened as possible.

"We have to make sure you're safe, for the baby's sake."

Elena smiled and thanked him, before looking down at the metallic seatbelt buckle uncomfortably pressed against her stomach.

15

Nearing the end of Elena's third month of pregnancy, everything had changed, just like Diego promised it would.

He cooked the food and washed the dishes. He swept the floors. He did the laundry. He dusted. He mopped. He cleaned the washroom. He brought Elena a pillow whenever she said she wasn't comfortable. Anything she would ask him to do, he did. It soon reached a point where she would spend most of her free time racking her brain trying to come up with new things to ask her husband to do, just to give herself something to do, as he never let her do anything that didn't involve him doing it for her. He was always there for her, even more than before when he was always there for her.

She now understood why Diego was not worried at all about her wearing the device while she was pregnant, and why he did not even bother acknowledging it back in the hospital. The possibility of ever being more than one hundred meters away from him was impossible, because other than going for her scheduled medical appointments, where Diego was never further than a few meters away from her, she never left the condo. Whenever they wanted food, he made a phone call and food arrived. Whenever they needed anything for the house, from fresh light bulbs to new sheets, he made a phone call and it arrived.

She often thought about the child. She envisioned feeding it, first from her breast, then from a bottle, then from a spoon. She thought about what the child would look like and what its personality would be. She could not wait to see what kind of father Diego would be.

After returning from the washroom for what had to be the tenth time that afternoon, Diego sat beside Elena and started rubbing her feet.

"Would you like to go out tonight?"

"Really?" she said. "Where?"

"I thought we could see a movie."

Surprised at the offer, but not wanting to risk missing out on it by hesitating, Elena immediately replied, "Yes, yes, I'd love to."

Diego released his grip on her foot. They both got up and made their way to the bedroom, but just as they reached the beginning of the hallway, she playfully pushed Diego aside and ran down the corridor until she reached the bedroom and declared herself the winner of the race. When she saw her husband's face, however, Elena was immediately beset with guilt and shame. Diego approached her. With every step, she felt worse as his expression grew more condemning. When he finally reached her, he said, "That was stupid what you did, Elena. What if you tripped? What if you slipped and hit the wall? You have to think about the baby. You have to be responsible. You have to be smart. Don't ever do anything like that again."

Elena lowered her head, said she was sorry multiple times, raised her head, and added, "You're right, that was stupid. I wasn't thinking. I won't do anything like that again, I'm so sorry."

Worried her actions may have jeopardized the opportunity to go out, she continued apologizing until Diego grabbed her shoulder, said he loved her, smiled, and said everything was okay before telling her one more time to never do anything like that again. Relieved, Elena nodded and followed her husband into the bedroom, where they both changed their clothes.

As the car approached the enormous movie theatre, Elena couldn't help but marvel at its majestic appearance in the same way she marveled at the shopping mall and the hospital. Diego parked the car as close to the theatre as he could, making sure his wife would not have to walk any more than she needed to.

There was a horde of people inside the building, huddled close, forming a loose line in front of a long counter where several employees stood and dispensed tickets.

"Which movie should we watch?" Elena asked.

"I was thinking we could watch that one over there," Diego replied, pointing at the largest of several posters dangling from the wall behind the counters.

Elena read the title and didn't recognize it, but she trusted Diego's judgment.

After Diego purchased the tickets, Elena wrapped both of her arms around his arm, pushed her body against it, and squeezed. He looked down at her, smiled, kissed her on the forehead, and said, "Down there, theatre number ten."

Holding hands, they walked into a large, dark room with an enormous grey, blank screen looming over them. Elena shivered as the room's air conditioning blasted against whatever skin she had left exposed.

"Can we sit in the back row?" she said.

"I prefer to sit in the front rows," Diego replied. "People are always talking in the back."

Elena nodded before they proceeded to the second row and sat in the centermost seats. She stared up at the blank screen and felt her neck immediately start to ache. Diego leaned back in his seat, contorting his body perfectly, allowing him to see the screen in its entirety without having to tilt his neck at all. Elena tried to mimic her husband's position, but just when she was about to achieve it, just when she felt the ache alleviate, Diego said, "Don't sit like that. It could affect the baby."

Not wishing to argue, feeling foolish for her selfishness and grateful Diego was so vigilant when it came to the baby's well-being, Elena sat straight and tilted her neck upwards, doing her best to ignore the reinvigorated ache. The entire room, now filled with people, went dark. The screen came to life, shining bright in the darkness. Booming music blasted from all sides.

During the first hour of the film, Elena had to go to the washroom twice, and because the washroom was on the other side of the building, Diego had to accompany her. She apologized both times, telling him she tried to hold it as long as she could. Each time he replied with a comforting smile.

By the time the film's ninetieth minute approached, Elena had to go to the washroom for the fourth time, and as she and her husband left the theatre and light enveloped them, Diego, no longer able to hide his aggravation, started scolding her, telling her that as a result of having to constantly walk with her to the washroom he was losing track of the film's plot. Elena pleaded with him, telling him it was out of her control. He nodded, said she was right, and apologized, before kissing her gently on the lips, which melted her heart and instilled a sense of determination that she would not interfere with her husband's enjoyment of the film again.

After the film's second hour, Elena's insides felt like they were being crushed by a clenching iron fist, but she refused to say anything. She refused to disturb her husband again. She refused to succumb to her weakness.

With barbs of pain bombarding her senses, she withered in her seat, squirming excessively, hoping the excessive movement would quell the desires of her bladder, but it was no use. She glanced at Diego and saw him staring at the bright screen, and with the pain finally proving too much, she wet herself.

After the film's credits started scrolling on the screen, the lights inside the room turned on. People were standing on both sides of Elena, jostling with each other in an attempt to exit the theatre as quickly as possible, but she remained seated, shrinking in her chair, staring at the floor.

"Excuse me," somebody beside her said.

She didn't reply. She just kept staring at the floor, hoping the person would go away.

"Elena, come on, let's go," Diego said.

Just as she did with the person who asked her to move a moment ago, she didn't respond. She just stayed where she was, staring at the floor, sitting in a pool of her urine.

She felt a hand grab and squeeze her shoulder.

"Elena, let's go."

She looked up and saw Diego staring back at her impatiently. She looked to the other side. The other person had already left, exiting the row from the other direction. The only people remaining in the row were her and her husband. Diego's hand clenched her shoulder even harder. She stood. Diego turned and started making his way down the row, while Elena remained where she was, staring down at the soaked seat, still feeling the humiliating warmth in her underwear and jeans.

With the room now completely illuminated, Diego stood at the end of the row, staring at his wife oddly. She glanced back down at the seat stained with her shame. Diego took a single step toward her. Terrified he would see what she had done, she stormed down the row toward him, but slipped and crashed into several seats, the handle of one seat striking her in the stomach. Diego gasped. Elena immediately got back up and ran right by him until she had immersed herself into the crowd of people trying to squeeze through the exit door.

When she finally made it through the door, Elena started making her way to the washroom on the other side of the building, hoping Diego was close behind. She did her best to tune out the noise from the crowd and listen for a beeping sound from the device. Unable to hear anything from the device, she continued toward the washroom but stopped when she started to feel pain in her ankle. She couldn't be sure but believed the device was squeezing it. Just as she was about to bend down and investigate, she felt a familiarly powerful hand grab and squeeze her shoulder. Knowing it was Diego's, she desperately searched for the washroom sign, hoping it was close. She spotted it, and it was well within one hundred meters. Without looking back or saying a word, she dashed to the washroom, went inside, and entered one of the vacant stalls.

After pulling down her dampened jeans and soaked underwear, she sat on the toilet seat. She grabbed the toilet paper and tugged at it until she had a thick wad. She started dabbing, rubbing, and wiping her inner thighs. After tossing the soiled paper into a garbage can, she grabbed and formed another wad and dabbed her underwear and jeans. While she managed to dry a great deal of her underwear, the denim of her jeans clung to the moisture, determined to remind her of her foul indiscretion. She stood, pulled her underwear and jeans back up, and once again felt the same humiliating warmth. When she exited the washroom, she saw Diego standing across the hallway, staring at her.

"What the hell is wrong with you? Why did you run down the aisle like that? Why did you run out of the theatre?"

"I'm sorry, Diego. I was embarrassed. I had to get out of there."

"Why? What happened?"

"I peed myself," she said, before lowering her head, dreading her husband's response.

There was a pause, and despite the noise from people walking throughout the theatre, all she heard was her husband's silence. She looked up and saw Diego looking around as if he were trying to see if anybody else had overheard her. He took three steps toward her and leaned close.

"Why would you do that?"

"I didn't want to disturb you during the movie again. I held it for as long as I could, but it started to hurt. I couldn't hold it anymore. It just happened."

Diego shook his head. Elena looked back down at the floor.

"If you have to go to the washroom, you go, Elena."

"But you looked like you were enjoying it, and I didn't want to ruin it for you."

"It's just a stupid movie. It wasn't worth you falling in the aisle while running like an idiot. You endangered the baby, Elena. What you did was stupid, just stupid."

"I'm sorry," she said. "I'm so sorry."

Diego turned around, but not before Elena noticed him glance at the front of her pants. She knew he saw the stains after seeing a brief, but an unmistakable look of disgust on his face. She bowed her head, unsure if she would ever be able to raise it again. When Diego started walking, she followed close behind, not saying a word.

After they left the building, Elena's head remained lowered. She looked at nothing but her feet, concealed ankles, and the ground while hoping Diego would lead her to where she needed to go. When she reached the car, she stopped and waited for him to open the door for her, just like he ever since her pregnancy was confirmed, but all she heard was the car's trunk pop open.

She raised her head and saw Diego leaning down, reaching into the trunk of the car, before standing back up with a large plastic sheet held firmly in his hands. After closing the trunk with a loud slam, he approached his wife. She took a step back, unsure what he was planning to do, but felt a wave of calm when she saw him open the passenger side door and place the sheet on the seat before thoroughly spreading it against the soft, leather upholstery.

16

"This happens much more than you know, Mr. Escobedo, especially during the first few months, but your wife is going to be just fine. She's very young and healthy. She should have no issues having children in the future."

Diego leaned back in his seat and replied, "I know exactly why this happened. I told her what she did last night was stupid."

"What happened last night?" the doctor said.

"She ran down one of the rows in a movie theatre, tripped, and hit her stomach against one of the chair handles."

Throughout the exchange, Elena's eyes were focused on the floor. She could not bear looking at her husband. She could not bear looking at the doctor, but she refused to close her eyes because every time they shut all she could see was the blood soaking and staining the bed. She vividly recalled the moisture that woke her up and how it was every bit as warm as what she felt in her underwear and jeans the night before in the movie theatre.

"I doubt that did it, Mr. Escobedo. I've seen women much further along than your wife get hit by cars, and their babies were born without any issues. As I said, you'd be surprised to hear how often this happens in the early stages of pregnancy."

Elena knew her husband was unconvinced, just by the intensity of his breathing.

"As I said, your wife is young and healthy and should have no problem having children in the future. You'll both be able to try again, soon."

"Thank you, Doctor," Diego said.

With Elena's eyes still focused on the floor, it wasn't until she felt her husband's hand grab and squeeze her shoulder that she looked up.

"Let's go."

Not a word was spoken during the drive home. Elena stared down at her feet. She refused to look through the window. She did not want to see the city passing her by. She did not want to see any of the cars. She did not want to see any of the people. She did not want to see any of the buildings. She did not want to see any of the parks.

It was not until the car came to a complete stop inside of the garage that she finally looked up, only to see Diego staring back at her. He looked broken and confused, like a child discovering death for the first time. She looked down at her ankle, hoping the device would explode and kill them both, simultaneously extinguishing her shame and his rage. She considered getting out of the car and running away, crossing the one-hundred-meter threshold as quickly as possible, knowing it would at least end her guilt, but the garage was too confined and did not offer her the space required.

After getting out of the car, Elena was not thinking about the baby she had lost, but about the husband she had lost. She did not believe he would care for her like he used to and comfort her like he used to. She doubted he would ever love her like he used to. She had no idea what kind of husband he was going to be.

After the condo's heavy front door slammed shut, she went to the master bedroom, but not before stopping in front of Diego's office, which was going to become the child's room. She glared at the door's handle but refused to touch it.

Inside the master bedroom, she sat on the bed. Diego walked in and closed the door. He looked like he was going to fall to his knees and cry, something she had never seen him do, something she didn't even know he could do.

"I know how hard this must be for you," he said, holding back the tears she expected to see at any moment, "but we have to move on from it. Just keep remembering what the doctor said, Elena, that you're young and healthy, and there will be lots of time for us to have more children. I know it wasn't your fault. I'm sorry for making it seem like it was. I just didn't know how to handle it. I still don't. I feel so empty right now."

Sitting on the bed, staring at her lamenting husband, Elena started to laugh without knowing why. Nonetheless, after a few seconds, her laughter grew hysterical. She couldn't stop. She had no control. She could barely breathe. Her laughter boomed throughout the room, while her cheekbones rose so high, they forced her eyes shut. She felt Diego's hands grasp her shoulders and the first thing she noticed was how feeble his grip was. She opened her eyes.

"What is wrong with you?" he said.

"I've never seen you so weak," she replied.

Breaking her husband's impotent grip, Elena let her body fall back atop the bed's recently replaced sheets. Feeling the mattress greet her, she raised and stretched her arms and legs. Diego took several timid steps back. The cuff of her jeans fell far enough to expose the device wrapped around her ankle. She stared at the device and saw the contrast between its fortitude and the fragility of the man who put it there.

She looked away from the device and gazed up at the ceiling. More laughter exploded from her mouth. Her entire body shook. Tears spilled from her eyes before rolling down the sides of her face. When her body could take no more, when her ribs ached and her throat clenched, the laughter finally, mercifully stopped.

Too exhausted to sit back up, she was startled by the sight of her husband leaning over her.

"I hope you enjoyed that," he said.

He thrust both of his hands toward her. She thought they were aimed at her throat. Still unable to move, she waited for whatever was to come, but was surprised when he gently wiped away what was left of the tears that had spilled from her eyes. The pressure of his thumbs against her face sent a surge throughout her body. Her fit of uncontrollable laughter became an afterthought.

Diego rose back up. Looking just as tall, just as strong, and just as powerful as ever, he loomed over her and extended his hand, which she immediately took, and with a commanding jerk, he pulled her toward him. With another equally authoritative tug, he pulled her up from the bed and hugged her, tight, and kissed her, hard, before releasing her, allowing her to take a free breath.

"I love you so much, Elena, and I will always love you, for the rest of your life."

Elena broke the embrace, pushed her husband away, reared her arm back, and with all her might thrust her hand, her arm, her shoulder, her entire body at him in a vicious slap that struck his face so hard the reverberation caused her teeth to clench. Afterward, she glared at her opened palm. It throbbed and glowed red. She looked at her husband.

He didn't charge at her, but she didn't expect him to. He didn't attempt to hit her back, but she didn't expect him to do that either. He didn't even verbally respond. He just smiled at her, while softly rubbing his cheek with his hand.

Angered by her husband's reaction, she reared back her unruly hand again and fired the swelling palm forward, striking him in the same spot on his face she struck just a few seconds earlier. The pain in her palm intensified. She took a step back and stared at the reddish handprint covering half of Diego's face.

"Are you finished?" he said.

"Why aren't you fighting back?"

"I don't need to. You had a lot to get out of your system, so I let you get it out. If that meant enduring a little pain to make you feel better, so be it. That's what love is, Elena."

The redness on Diego's face started to subside and his skin's fair complexion returned.

"I don't understand," she said.

"Sometimes, I forget how young you are."

"But why were you smiling? Didn't it hurt?"

"You could never hurt me."

She looked down at her hand and turned it over, and even though the redness on her husband's face had all but disappeared, the redness on her palm not only remained but grew more intense. She looked back at Diego without speaking.

"And I was smiling because I was happy to see you release all of the anger, the sadness, the regret I know you've been feeling ever since you lost the baby."

"Even if that meant hitting you?" she said.

"Yes."

"I can't stand you," she shouted.

"Why? I allowed you to laugh in my face, insult me, even hit me, twice, and I'm the one you can't stand?"

Elena closed her eyes and wished Diego would have pulled his arm back and thrust it forward, striking her hard enough to knock her to the other side of the room. She envisioned blood spilling from her nose and the skin surrounding both of her eyes turning purple. But when she opened her eyes and caressed her cheek, she felt nothing but the disappointing softness of her hand.

"I'm leaving," she said.

Diego stepped aside, but she remained where she was.

"What are you waiting for?"

Elena didn't move a muscle or say a word.

"Oh, I get it," he said. "How can you leave with nothing to leave with?"

He walked to the closet, reached up, and effortlessly pulled out Elena's shabby suitcase. He slammed it on the bed and asked her what she wanted to pack. Elena didn't respond. She just stared at the exhausted-looking piece of luggage then glanced down at her ankle.

"You know I can't leave."

Diego approached his wife, raised both his hands, rested them on each one of her shoulders, held them firm, looked down, and said, "Now that we've established that you're not going anywhere, I suggest you lie down and get some rest. You've been through a lot today."

Diego grabbed the suitcase, flung it back on the closet's top shelf, and pushed it as far back as he could until it was completely out of sight before walking out of the closet and leaving the room.

After Elena heard the washroom door open and close, she went into the closet. Pushing aside all of the articles of clothing Diego had purchased for her, she stood as tall as she could, but could not see the suitcase. She shut her eyes and imagined herself grabbing it and confidently slamming it on the bed. She saw herself throwing all of the dresses her mother made for her inside, ignoring the jeans and t-shirts her husband bought for her, while triumphantly telling him she was leaving him, but when she opened her eyes, all she could see were pairs of jeans dangling from their hangers.

She retreated to the bed, cowered underneath the comforter, and grabbed a pillow. Elena felt herself fading into sleep, but her escape was foiled when the comforter was abruptly torn away from her. She looked up and saw Diego standing over her. He had no shirt on, and a towel wrapped around his waist.

"Are you okay?"

Elena didn't reply. She stared at his body. Drops of water rolled down his chest and arms. His skin glistened. She grabbed him and wrapped her arms around him. Surprised at her strength, she pulled him down to the bed. He collapsed atop the mattress. With her arms still tightly clamped around his body, she squeezed as hard as she could. She pressed her face against his chest.

Diego wrapped his arms around her. Feeling his strong hands, she raised her head and stared at his face. She looked him in the eye, breathed through her nose, smelled the fragrance of his freshly cleansed body, and kissed him. Her first kiss was soft and tender, but every subsequent kiss grew more aggressive until her jaw started to ache. She twisted and pushed Diego flat on the bed. She tore the towel off his waist, revealing the rest of his physique, while his arms lay flat on the mattress.

Elena peeled off her clothes, tossing her shirt, jeans, underwear, and socks to every corner of the bedroom. With nothing on but the device clamped around her ankle, she wrapped her thighs around him, squeezing as hard as she could. He attempted to adjust his position, but she squeezed her legs tighter, forcing him to remain exactly where he was. She thrust herself upon him, pushing him as deeply into her as she could. His initial sounds of guarded pleasure made way for uncontrollable moans, but she refused to loosen her grip.

After her husband climaxed, Elena kept going, even faster and harder than before. Diego, whose entire body became one big contracting spasm, wrapped his arms around his wife's madly moving hips and managed to raise her off of him and toss her to the other side of the bed. Staring at the ceiling, Elena placed her sweaty palms on her strained abdominal muscles and took a series of short breaths that whistled between her trembling lips. She got off the bed and put her clothes back on, while Diego remained on the bed, breathing deep, exhausted breaths. She left the bedroom, walked into the washroom, turned on the light, and saw traces of blood on her bottom lip. She had kissed Diego so hard she had cut it. After washing her face and hands, Elena left the washroom and walked down the hallway until she reached the condo's front door.

After she opened the heavy door, a rush of air from the hallway snuck through the narrow crevice and brushed against her cheek. Elena looked behind her but did not see Diego, whom she hoped remained in the bedroom, on the bed, still panting with fatigue. She opened the door wider, exposing her entire body to the hallway. The gust of air grew stronger, grazing her entire figure. While still firmly holding the door open, she poked her head out, looked in both directions, and saw nobody. She then fixated on the elevator at the end of the hall. It was the perfect place because when it eventually crossed the one-hundred-meter threshold, Elena believed the enclosed nature of the elevator's interior would be able to contain the explosion, ensuring nobody else got hurt.

She suddenly felt the device squeeze her ankle just like she thought it did in the movie theatre. Knowing that just a single step was all she had to take to exit the condo completely, something she had never done without Diego, she ignored the sudden influx of pain, believing it was all in her head, a figment of her fear.

Still standing in the doorway, trembling, breathing rapidly, as if she were standing at the edge of a cliff, Elena turned and glanced back into the condo. When she heard the door of the master bedroom open and shut, she turned back around, closed her eyes, and stepped into the hallway. She immediately felt a rush of pain stemming from the device. She opened her eyes and exhaled but jumped when she heard the condo's heavy front door slam behind her. Standing in the hallway, the pain in her ankle grew worse until it became unbearable. It wasn't a figment of her fear. The device was squeezing her ankle.

She stared at the elevator and debated whether or not to take a step toward it when the front door of the condo swung open. She spun around and saw Diego standing naked in the doorway. He reached out and wrapped his arms around her. With his arms securely enveloping her, he pulled her back into the security of the condo.

17

Elena walked into the cafe, saw Ana and Maria seated at a table near the back, and marched toward them. Ana saw her first, Maria noticed her a moment later.

"Wow," Maria said. "You look great.

"It's true," Ana said. "You look like you lost even more weight."

Elena didn't respond, but she knew Ana was right. She had lost a great deal of weight following the collapse of her pregnancy. Her engagement ring, wedding ring, jeans, and even the device itself, felt looser and regrettably more comfortable.

She glanced at the vacant chair on the other side of the small table but had no intention of sitting on it. She glanced at Diego, who had taken a seat at a table a few meters away. She turned back around and saw expressions of curiosity on Ana and Maria's faces. She bent down, grabbed the left cuff of her jeans, and raised it high, revealing the device.

She looked up.

"Oh my God," Ana said, "I can't believe you have a device. I've always dreamed of having one of those."

Elena released the cuff of her jeans, allowing it to fall back down. She felt her throat contract, making it difficult for her to swallow the words she had just heard. After several attempts, she managed to clear her throat before replying, "What are you talking about?"

"You're the first woman I know to have one," Maria said.

"Only the lucky ones get devices," Ana said.

"But it's a bomb," Elena shouted.

She expected the entire cafe to go silent, for all of the surrounding chatter to cease, and for all eyes to focus on her, but despite how fearful and how loud her words were, not a single conversation paused, and not a single person, except for Ana and Maria, even bothered to offer her a glance, not even Diego.

She stumbled to the vacant chair and sat. Her face clenched. She couldn't speak.

"Can I see it again?" Ana said.

Maria seconded the request. In a daze, Elena leaned forward and raised the cuff of her jeans.

Ana shook her head and said, "I thought you were lucky before, but after finding out your husband put a device around your ankle, and that he did it so soon. I don't even know what to call that."

"Neither do I," Elena said.

"Don't you know what this means?" Maria said.

"Yes," Elena replied, "that I have a bomb on my ankle."

"It means you found a man who loves you so much he wants to keep you within one-hundred meters of him, all the time, for the rest of your life."

"I wish I was you right now," Ana said.

Elena didn't respond. She couldn't respond. She started looking around, waiting, hoping for a sign, a sound, a sight, something, anything that would confirm she was either dreaming or had gone mad.

"He'll always be faithful to you," Maria said, "because it's not like he can ever cheat on you now."

Ana turned toward Maria and said, "I heard about one guy who bought his wife a device and still cheated on her."

Maria turned back toward Ana and replied, "Really? How? Anyway, I don't think Diego is that kind of guy though, not after buying her one this soon."

After accepting she was not dreaming and had not gone mad, that what was happening was happening, and what she was hearing was being said, Elena turned around and looked at her husband sitting at the table he said he would occupy as soon as they walked in. He smiled at her.

"Can I see it again," Ana said.

Maria turned to Ana, laughed, and said, "You've already seen it twice."

"It's just so amazing," Ana said. "Don't act like you don't want to see it again, too."

Maria didn't reply, but after looking at her face, Elena knew it was true, so she knelt, grabbed the cuff of her jeans, and raised it again. Afterward, Elena leaned back in her chair and noticed two girls seated at a table to her left leering at her enviously.

"When did he put it on you?" Maria asked.

"On our wedding night, after I fell asleep," Elena replied. "I woke up and there it was."

"Oh my God," Ana said, "that is the most romantic thing I've ever heard."

"At first I thought it was a joke," Elena said, "then it started scaring me because I couldn't believe something like that existed. I still can't believe it."

"That's what makes the device so amazing," Maria said. "They're almost impossible to get. You have to find a broker just to set up the deal to buy one."

"I can't believe he gave it to you after only being with you for a few weeks," Ana said.

Elena noticed Ana glance at Diego.

"It's the ultimate symbol of love," Maria said.

"How is that?" Elena asked.

"Because once the device is put on, it can never be taken off," Maria replied. "Engagement rings are nice, and the one Diego got you is beautiful, but nothing proves a husband's love like a device."

Elena shook her head and said, "If they're so amazing, why is it that when I saw the doctor for an exam a few months ago, he acted like the device wasn't even there? I started to think it was all in my head, that maybe the device wasn't real, that I was going crazy."

Ana laughed, irritating Elena, while Maria replied, "Which hospital did you go to?"

Confused by the question, Elena, while forgetting the exact name of the hospital, said it had the word angel in it.

Both Ana and Maria looked at each other, and exchanged smiles, further compounding Elena's confusion, before Maria turned back to her and said, "That's one of the best, most exclusive hospitals in the city."

"And the only men who can afford to take their wives to that hospital, are the ones who buy them devices," Ana added. Men who truly love their wives would never take them to those disgusting public hospitals."

Elena noticed Ana shaking her head, muttering to herself.

"It's probably like seeing a piece of jewelry," Maria said. "I bet the doctor didn't say anything about your engagement ring either."

Elena didn't know what to say or what to think. She looked at her engagement ring before gripping it with her fingers and rotating it around and around, while never taking her eyes off the diamond.

"Why did you have to get an exam?" Maria asked.

"I was pregnant," she replied.

Ana gasped, but Elena could not tell if she was excited or upset. It was not until she said the word miscarriage that Ana's face calmed.

"I'm sorry," Maria said.

"Yeah," Ana said, "me, too."

Elena shifted her posture before leaning forward. She looked around again, still curious if anybody else was listening to the conversation.

"What would have happened if I went through the full pregnancy?"

"What do you mean?" Maria asked.

"If I went through the full pregnancy and gained the weight women typically gain, what would have happened with the device? It's comfortable now, but I know if I gained any weight, it would be too tight."

"The device is designed to adapt to your ideal pregnancy weight," Maria said. "It expands just enough to remain comfortable throughout your pregnancy, and I think three months after."

Ana shook her head, and said, "I heard it was only two months."

"What do you mean by ideal pregnancy weight?" Elena asked.

Ana turned to Elena, smiled, raised her hands and formed a large, invisible circle, and said, "It stops you from blowing up like a balloon."

"But what happens if you can't help but gain weight?"

Elena cringed at the possible answer but wanted to know.

"Once the device senses your body has reached its maximum allowable weight gain," Maria said, "it stops expanding, which of course causes a lot of pain, pain that just gets worse the more weight you gain, forcing you to lose the weight as quickly as possible."

"I love it," Ana said. "The device makes sure you stay in shape for the rest of your life. Now we know your secret, Elena. Now we know how you've been losing all of that weight."

"The device is amazing," Maria said. "That's why it costs so much. That's why so many guys don't get it for their wives, or can't get it, or don't want to get it because it's such a huge investment. And since you can't take it off once it's put on, it has to be paid for upfront. I've heard stories about guys saving for the first ten years of their marriage before they could afford to get one for their wives."

"And Diego got one for you on your wedding night, after only knowing you for a few weeks," Ana said. "I've never heard of a man loving a woman that much, that fast."

Elena continued asking questions about the device, and Ana and Maria were more than happy to answer them as if talking about the device allowed them to vicariously have one clamped around their ankles. She asked them if there were any stories about women putting devices on their husbands' ankles, but before either Ana or Maria answered, another, more pressing question suddenly rushed to the forefront of her mind.

"Have either of you heard about one of the devices exploding?"

"What do you mean?" Ana said.

"I was inside of a shopping mall with Diego, and I lost track of where he was, and there were so many people around me. I started to freak out and I ran after him just to catch up to him. The whole time I kept wondering how big the explosion would be, and how many people near me it would kill. That's when I knew I could never take the risk. So I want to know if either of you knows about any devices exploding?"

Both Ana and Maria looked at each other, shook their heads, and turned back toward Elena.

"No," Maria said.

"No," Ana said.

Elena leaned back in her chair, "So there has never been a case of a woman wearing one of these devices who crossed the line?"

"Why would anybody cross the line when they know the device will explode?" Ana said. "Plus, I heard it starts to beep once you get close to the one-hundred meters, so it's not like a woman wouldn't know if they were too far away and had to run back to their husband."

"But how do we know they even explode if it has never happened?"

"You know because it has never happened," Maria said.

"Exactly," Ana added.

"But how can so many women in a city this populated be allowed to have something on them that could kill innocent people?"

"But there aren't many women wearing those devices," Maria said.

"Okay, okay," Elena said, "fine, but even if it's just a few women, how can it be legal to have something on you that could potentially kill innocent people at any time in any place?"

"It's legal to carry guns in other countries, and those can kill innocent people at any time, in any place," Ana said. "I heard in some countries people can bring their guns into shopping malls, bars, churches, even universities, so what's the difference?"

Elena didn't know what to say.

"One hundred meters is such a huge distance anyway, so why worry?" Maria said. "I doubt I'd ever be that far away from my husband even if I didn't have a device on my ankle."

"Yeah," Ana said, "It's not like the limit is fifty meters. That would just be crazy."

Elena glanced at Ana, who started shaking her head. She questioned her as to why she was doing it.

Ana stopped shaking her head and replied, "Nothing, nothing. I just can't believe how amazing that device is. I just hope I get one put on my ankle someday."

Elena noticed Ana had snuck yet another glance at Diego.

"They keep you safe, too," Maria said.

"What?" Elena said, reluctantly turning her attention away from Ana.

"I read that ever since the devices were introduced a few years ago, kidnappings of rich guys' wives have decreased by over eighty percent."

"Why?" Elena said.

"Once kidnappers found out a man had money, and if he had no kids, they would target the wife, grab her and take her somewhere before demanding a ransom. But now, because of the devices, they can't do that because the minute they get more than one hundred meters away from the husband, the kidnappers would get blown up."

"But so would the wife," Elena said.

"Yeah, but the kidnappers value their lives more than the wife's," Maria replied.

"What if they just kidnap the husband and wife at the same time and keep them together?" Elena asked.

"Then who would be able to pay the ransom?" Ana said.

"If it keeps me so safe," Elena said, "why is Diego obsessed with me covering it up? Why did he make sure I was always wearing these jeans instead of the dresses my mom made for me? Why do I always have to keep it covered?"

"Maybe he wants you to keep it covered so it will be more personal," Maria said, "so he can keep it just between the two of you. There are a lot of jealous people out there, Elena."

Elena leaned forward, peered down at the concealed device, and said, "I remember walking out of the condo, by myself, and even though I was well within one hundred meters of Diego, the device started squeezing. I thought it was in my head, but it felt so real. It happened in a movie theatre, too, but it didn't hurt nearly as much as it did in the condo."

"What were you thinking about doing when you walked out of the condo?" Maria asked.

Elena sat back up, looked at Maria, and said, "What do you mean?"

"Were you thinking about leaving him?"

Unsure how to respond, Elena shook her head and said no over and over again, capping off the final utterance by adding, "Of course not."

Glaring at her with an expression of fierce suspicion that made Elena wish she were anywhere but there, Ana said, "Are you sure?"

"I, I don't think I was seriously considering it," Elena said. "I was going through a lot. I wasn't thinking straight. I didn't know what I was thinking."

"The device did," Maria said.

Elena's heart skipped a beat. She stared at Maria and said, "What are you talking about?"

"It's a smart device," Ana said.

"What does that mean?" Elena replied.

"It's just like our phones, but even more advanced. I heard it can read brain impulses or something like that, I'm not exactly sure," Maria said, "but it senses when a woman is panicking or thinking about breaking the one-hundred meters, and when it thinks she is, the device squeezes to clear her mind, letting her know she should not do whatever it is she's thinking about doing."

"It kickstarts the brain," Ana said, "so the woman wearing it can think straight again."

"So, the device protects itself?" Elena said.

"Of course not, it's just a device, why would it care about protecting itself?" Ana replied. "It was protecting you. I told you, we told you, that device wrapped around your ankle is incredible. It's perfect."

"I read that it's made out of the same metal they use to build space shuttles," Maria said, "so it will never crack or dent."

"I heard it doesn't even rust," Ana added.

"It doesn't," Elena said.

Without looking down, Elena raised the cuff of her jeans, reared back her left leg, and slammed the device against the thick, single leg of the table. Both Ana and Maria jumped from their seats as the table shook with stress. Looking around the cafe, curious to see if any of the other customers noticed what she had done, Elena just shook her head when her action inspired the same apathy she witnessed after first revealing the device.

Elena, Ana, and Maria leaned forward and gazed at the device. It did not suffer a single scratch. Elena closed her eyes while Ana and Maria clapped their hands, applauding its invincibility.

18

Elena was watching a soap opera when Diego stepped in front of the television.

"I have a surprise for you."

She sank deep into the sofa's cushions, terrified of what new surprise her husband could have in store for her.

"I'm taking us for a vacation, to a resort. We leave tomorrow morning. It's all set up. I got a great deal. It was almost too good to be true. I thought it would be the perfect gift for our wedding anniversary."

The next day, when Elena woke up, Diego was already dressed and packing his suitcase. She glanced at the shrouded window and saw nothing but darkness.

"What time is it?"

"It's early, but if you want to get out of the city without having to spend hours in traffic, you have to leave when it's still dark."

Turning over in the bed, she watched Diego walk into the closet and pull out her old, battered suitcase. After tossing the suitcase on the bed, Diego opened it, revealing its empty interior before looking at his wife, who remained on the bed. He told her to pack for a week.

Elena rolled out of bed, approached the closet, stopped, turned back toward Diego, and asked him what she should pack.

"It's going to be hot," he said, "and humid."

She mentioned the possibility of bringing the dresses her mother made for her.

"I threw those out months ago," he replied. "I thought I told you?"

Elena lowered her head, mourning the loss, before telling him that since her dresses were gone, she didn't have anything to wear for hot, humid weather. Diego looked back down at the empty, battered suitcase and closed it back up.

"Don't worry about it," he said. "I'll just buy you some new clothes when we get there. I'm going to throw this suitcase out, too. It looks awful and isn't worth keeping. I'll just buy you a new one."

After she showered and put on a grey t-shirt, socks, and a pair of jeans, Elena walked into the living room and saw her husband on the couch, fidgeting like a child next to his beautiful suitcase.

"Are you ready?" he said.

Empty-handed, with nothing even in her pockets, Elena said she was.

With the sun still slumbering, Diego was able to make his way through the city's streets with ease. As they left the capital, Elena turned around expecting to see the city's lights, but the sun had already started to rise, and its rays doused their shine. When she turned back around, her body tensed. Diego was driving her into the same bleak, dark area she passed through when she first arrived at the capital. With the sun shining brighter, however, the area she initially deemed too frightening to step foot in was now so illuminated Elena had to put on the oversized sunglasses Diego bought for her. And while her surroundings still looked grim, they didn't appear much different from the city she now called home.

Hours later, after rows of despondent grey buildings lining both sides of the highway made way for empty wooden shacks, a car approached from behind before recklessly passing Diego's car. Diego didn't seem to notice the vehicle as it raced away, but Elena couldn't help but think about how close the car came to striking them.

"Diego, what would happen to me if something happened to you, like if you were killed in a car accident?"

With his eyes focused on the road ahead, Diego replied, "If I was in a car accident, you'd be right there with me."

"But what if I survived?"

Diego didn't respond.

"What if you were hit by a car while walking down the street?"

"You'd be by my side."

"But what if I survived?"

Not bothering to wait for a response, Elena continued, "What if you got sick and died?"

"If anything like that happened, you would be by my side to the very end."

"But what if it was sudden? What if you never saw it coming? What if you weren't given any time to prepare for it? What would happen to me? What would happen with the device?"

"You shouldn't be thinking about things like that, Elena. I've taken all the necessary steps in case something like that ever happened. You have nothing to worry about. All you need to know is I love you."

"But Diego--"

"We need gas," he said, cutting her off.

Diego pulled the car into a gas station.

As a young man with sun-worn skin pumped the gas, Elena got out of the car, stretched her lean limbs, and was greeted with an embrace of humidity that immediately caused her jeans to cling to her legs, while her exposed skin started bubbling with sweat. She took off her sunglasses, wiped the sweat from her face, put the glasses back on, and looked around. She spotted a shabby building topped with a thin tin roof that did not appear capable of enduring the weakest of winds or softest of downpours.

She walked toward the building, knowing she'd be well within one hundred meters of Diego. Instead of chairs, there were small plastic stools lined up in front of a large square opening. Smoke blew out of the opening, and as Elena got closer, she was able to inhale the scent and instantly recalled a similar aroma from her hometown. She no longer walked, but ran toward the tiny restaurant, but stopped after she felt a sudden surge of pain from her ankle. She turned around and saw Diego standing by the car, staring at her. She shouted for him to follow her. After paying the attendant for the gas, he got back in the car and drove toward her. She stayed where she was and waited for him. The pain in her ankle disappeared. Together they walked to the restaurant.

Through the square opening of the restaurant, Elena saw a large dark-skinned man wearing a filthy, oversized apron. Behind the man was a short woman whose back was turned as she prepared the food. Elena sat on one of the stools. Diego sat beside her, doing absolutely nothing to hide his disgust with everything around him. The large man inside the restaurant, who had a collection of deep creases running throughout his face and forehead, looked at them and smiled, revealing several glinting metal teeth.

The man handed them a pair of menus. Diego reluctantly accepted one of the grease-stained menus with his thumb and forefinger, while Elena grabbed the other one with both of her hands. She eagerly read through it, recognizing every single item available.

"What would you like?" the man with the apron said.

Elena couldn't make up her mind. She wanted everything.

"Are you going to order something from here?" Diego said.

" It reminds me of home, Diego. You used to bring me food like this when we first met, remember?"

"I do, but I got that from a place I trusted in the city. That's why it cost so much. This food might make us sick, and the whole vacation would be ruined. Look at these menus, Elena. If they look like this, I can't imagine how bad the food is. Listen, we're not far from the hotel. We'll be there soon, and then we can eat. I promise."

Elena looked up, saw the face of the large man in the apron, and realized he had heard every single word Diego had said, and while Elena couldn't see the face of the woman cooking in the back of the restaurant, she did notice her momentarily stop preparing it, while bowing her head. Unable to stand the shame, Elena told her husband to buy a bottle of soda for her. After he agreed, she got up from the stool, asked him for the car keys, and without looking back, too ashamed to look back, she returned to the car.

When they reached a small highway town that uncannily resembled her hometown, Diego steered the car off the highway and immersed the vehicle into it. He weaved through the sleepy town's narrow, bumpy, burdened streets. Elena stared through the window, feeling as if she were going back in time.

She saw two men sitting on a small staircase in front of a building on the verge of collapse, saying nothing to each other, while staring at a large pothole filled with muddy water. She saw a group of children and elderly people huddled around several metal garbage cans, while reaching in and pulling out aluminum cans and glass bottles. She saw people roaming the streets, walking listlessly. They had dark, haggard faces and red, tired eyes. Not many people looked up from the ground as they walked, but the few who did saw Diego's luxurious car and responded with scornfully curled lips.

After leaving the town behind, Diego started driving on a smooth, perfectly paved road. There was thick foliage on both sides as if the road cut right through a lush jungle. When the car reached the end of the road, Elena saw a gigantic marble fountain spewing water from several spouts. Behind the fountain was an enormous, sealed gate, and above the gate was a dazzling sign that read, *Welcome to Heaven.*

Elena wondered if the extravagance of the resort's front entrance made the small town they just drove through appear more decrepit than it was, or if the moribund state of the town made the entrance of the resort appear more extravagant than it was. She was still pondering when Diego drove up beside a small booth in front of the resort's gigantic gate.

"Hello, and welcome to Heaven."

The voice belonged to a young man in a khaki uniform. He had a dark complexion, similar to those of the people living in the small town, but unlike them, he had a big smile on his face. Diego told the young man his name. The man proceeded to look at a sheet of paper fastened to a clipboard, nodded, looked back up, pressed a button that opened the gate, and with a sweep of his arm permitted Diego to pass through the gate and enter heaven.

When they finally reached the hotel, the car stopped in front of the building. Elena opened the door and was instantly reacquainted with the muggy air. When she stepped out of the vehicle, sweat already soaking her arms, she watched Diego hand the car keys to another young man in a khaki uniform.

"What about your suitcase?" Elena asked.

"Don't worry about that," Diego said. "They'll bring it to the room. Let's just get inside. This humidity is horrible."

She followed her husband inside the hotel, and as soon as the glass doors closed behind her, she immediately felt cooled and comforted by the hotel's air conditioning. The interior was incredible. Elena's eyes were overloaded with colors and designs adorning the walls, floors, fountains, chairs, tables, and even the ceiling above.

Once they reached their room on the nineteenth floor, Diego opened the door and allowed Elena to enter first. The first thing she saw were two white, see-through curtains hanging above a large balcony doorway, blown inward by the warm wind. She turned and saw an enormous bed, even bigger than the one she shared with her husband. In the center of the bedspread was a collection of red rose petals positioned to look like a heart, but the wind had moved several of them around, disfiguring the shape. Next to the bed was a marble-topped table, where a sweating steel bucket was filled with ice and a bottle of champagne. Beside the bucket was a wicker basket filled with fresh fruit.

"Check out the balcony," Diego said, pointing toward the softly breathing curtains that formed unique, beautiful shapes with every gust.

Elena walked toward the doorway and tried to sweep the curtains aside, but they wrapped themselves around her, forcing her to contort her body just to break free of them. Once she escaped the curtains, she stepped onto the balcony and her eyes immediately focused on the ocean's stunning turquoise water. Diego joined his wife, wrapped his arms around her, and said, "You've never seen the ocean before, have you?"

Elena said no.

Diego smiled.

"That's why I brought us here. I wanted you to finally see it, and I wanted to be the one to show it to you."

Without looking away, enchanted by the ocean's allure and grandeur, she said, "Thank you, Diego. It's beautiful. I love it."

"The sun should be setting soon," he said.

"Can we see it from here?"

"Of course," he replied, "but look at this."

She turned and saw a circular tub filled with colorless water that churned and bubbled.

"It's a hot tub," he said.

She was unimpressed with the enclosed tub, especially when compared to the magnificence of the ocean. She had no interest in getting inside a giant porcelain pot filled with what looked like boiling water.

"Can we watch the sunset from the beach down there instead?" she asked. "I want to feel the ocean's water on my feet."

"I think the view of the sunset from up here will be better," Diego replied. "That's why I requested a room so high up, and why I got the hot tub so we could sit and relax without having to worry."

Elena leaned over the balcony's railing, gazing not just at the ocean beyond, but the concrete below.

"Worry about what?"

"The ocean is dangerous, Elena. There are waves, rocks, and the tide. This way you won't have to worry about the salt stinging your eyes or drying out your skin and hair."

Elena pulled herself back from the railing, but not before catching another glimpse of the ocean. She glared at her husband.

"But it's so beautiful, Diego. It's the most beautiful thing I've ever seen."

"I'll tell you what," he replied, "tomorrow morning we'll talk a long walk on the boardwalk down there, right by the beach, so you can see the ocean up close."

"I don't just want to see it. I want to feel the waves splashing against my feet, my legs, my ankles."

"I know they don't look that dangerous from up here, but if one of those waves grabs you it will pull you under and take you away, and before you know it, you'll be too far. I can't take that risk."

"So, this is about the device?"

Before he could respond, Elena's eyes moved away from his and gazed back at the ocean.

"I never even wanted this stupid device on my ankle. I never asked for it. You just put it on me."

Unwilling to turn away from the gorgeous, vast ocean beyond, Elena was unable to tell if Diego was upset, confused, hurt, or shocked. She waited for his response. After taking several seconds to find what she assumed were the right words, he finally replied.

"When I bought you those sunglasses, you didn't ask for them, but you accepted them and said you loved them, same thing with your cell phone and that new watch. And what about that engagement ring on your finger? You didn't ask for that either, but you accepted it and said you loved it. You accepted every gift I gave you, Elena, every single one, and said you loved it, so why would I think the device would be any different? I told you after we got married that you were no longer a princess; that you were a queen, and that device, that perfect device comfortably wrapped around your ankle, is what queens get."

Elena's hips were devoid of shape. Her thighs were powerless. Her stomach looked gaunt. Her breasts were drained. Her arms were stringy. Her skin was pale. She looked down and stared at the device, marveling at its immunity to the passing of time. She imagined the condition of the device in five years, ten years, thirty years, fifty, knowing it would remain perfect. She then imagined herself over those same fifty years and trembled, realizing how much she had deteriorated throughout just one.

She turned off the water, stepped out of the shower, and dried herself using a large white towel with the word heaven stitched in the center. When she left the washroom, she put on the same grey shirt and jeans she had on when she arrived the day before, as Diego had yet to take her shopping for clothes

Diego started stirring in the bed. When his eyes opened, he smiled at her.

"Why haven't we seen my mother yet, Diego? You promised we would."

"I know," he replied, "and I plan on keeping that promise, but I said we would when the time was right."

She glanced at the curtains breathing deeply.

"I want to go," she said.

Diego got out of bed, told his wife he was going to shower, and would be ready shortly.

"Did you want to get some food before we went out?"

"No," she replied, "I want to go now."

After Diego came out of the washroom he got dressed and told Elena he was ready. After the elevator ride to the main floor of the hotel, Diego approached the reception desk and asked the concierge how to get to the boardwalk he saw from the balcony. The concierge told him the boardwalk was outside of the resort's property and was unmonitored by the resort's security personnel, so the resort could not be held responsible if something happened. Diego turned to his wife and said, "Why don't we just get some breakfast and relax in the hot tub, and we can see the ocean from the balcony?"

"I want to go," she replied.

Diego sighed, "Are you sure?"

"Yes. I'm ready to go now."

Diego turned back to the concierge and repeated his question.

The concierge pulled out a small piece of paper and wrote down the instructions on how to get to the public boardwalk.

The walk to the resort's rear gate took ten minutes. Never more than a few meters behind her husband, Elena was constantly looking around, trying to see the impressive and verdant flora she remembered seeing when they drove to the front gate, but her view was obstructed by an enormous wall that appeared to encase the entire resort.

After exiting the secure grounds of the resort, Diego pulled out the small piece of paper the concierge gave him.

"This way," he said.

When they finally reached the public boardwalk, Elena could hear the ocean's water caressing the beach. She started walking faster, her shoes slamming on the boardwalk's wooden planks, and was just about to pass Diego, when he grabbed her hand, slowing her pace.

"Look at all we've been through in just one year, Elena. I know there have been some tough stretches, but I want you to know that business is great. Money is going to start flowing in, so I can buy all of the things you could ever want, better clothes, better shoes, a nicer watch, a nicer purse, a new cell phone, more vacations like this one, anything you want. Things will be even better than before. I promise."

She pulled her hand from her husband's grip and started rapidly walking down the boardwalk. She glanced back. Diego had picked up his pace and was just about to catch up to her. She walked even faster. Diego quickened his pace even more and was steps away from catching up to her. She turned and told him she wanted to run.

"In this heat?"

She nodded.

After a few minutes of running, Diego's pace started to slow. "It's too hot," he said. "Why don't we head back to the hotel and get some good food. After that, we can sit in the hot tub and look at the ocean."

Elena slowed. Diego stopped and grabbed her hand, halting her with a jerk. His eyes were full of love and his smile was full of joy.

"Happy Anniversary, Elena."

He raised his wife's left hand and pressed his lips against the knuckle below the two rings wrapped around her finger.

As soon as Elena felt Diego release her hand, she started walking again. Diego followed. She walked faster. Diego matched her pace.

"I want to run again," she said.

"It's too hot," he replied.

"I don't care."

She started running.

The gap between her and her husband widened. She felt a pinch from her ankle. She stopped and turned around, only to see Diego standing where he was, a bewildered look on his face. She turned back around and started to run again, widening the gap even more. The device reacted more angrily and what was once a slight pinch had become a painful surge she could feel in her fingertips. She stopped again and turned around. Diego still hadn't moved, and along with the bewilderment on his face, she believed she saw, for the first time since the device had been clamped around her ankle, genuine concern at the distance between them.

She took a step toward him and immediately felt the pain from the device diminish. But just as she was about to take another step, she heard him whistle at her while raising his hand and gesturing for her to come back as if she were a beloved, but disobedient dog. She stopped, turned back around, and despite the device's reinvigorated anger, she walked on, stretching the distance between her and her husband even more. Staring at the wooden planks beneath her feet, using them as a rudimentary means of measurement, she estimated she was thirty meters away from him when she started to run again. The pain from the device reached levels she had never felt before, but Elena continued running.

When the distance between her and Diego reached what she believed to be approximately sixty meters, she stopped running and turned around, but this time she had no thoughts of going back to him. He formed a circle with his hands, placed it around his mouth, and shouted, "Don't do it, Elena. Just come back and everything will be perfect. Whatever you want. I promise."

She looked down at the device concealed by her sweat-soaked jeans. She looked around and saw nobody anywhere near her. She looked back at Diego. He lowered his hands and started shaking his head. She wondered what he was thinking about, what he was feeling, before realizing she no longer cared.

Elena turned back around and continued running. She took off her sunglasses and tossed them aside before gazing at the gorgeous sun. Without breaking stride she unclasped her watch and threw it, not caring where it landed. Her thighs throbbed and her body started to cramp. The merciless device started squeezing so hard she felt her bones bend, believing they would snap at any moment, but she kept on running. Elena tried to remove her engagement ring and wedding ring, but it was no use, they were too tight. The device started beeping loudly while squeezing her ankle even harder. Tears streamed from her eyes, and despite the excruciating pain and piercing noise, a smile spread across her face just as she crossed the one-hundred-meter threshold.

She was free.

Acknowledgments

I want to thank Charlie Franco from Montag Press not only for your wonderful edits, but also for believing in this book, like you believed in my two previous books. Your belief in my work has meant a great deal to me, and I will always appreciate it. I want to thank John Rak for his insightful and helpful edits that made this story into what I always hoped it could be. And I want to thank *Arévalo_art* for creating a magnificent cover, muchisimas gracias!

Born and raised in Scarborough, Ontario, Canada, Jonathan R. Rose has always been surrounded by different cultural perspectives and experiences, which inspired his love of learning and travel. As a result, he has spent more than a third of his life in other countries, including Mexico, where he lived for almost 10 years.

Wedlock is Jonathan's third novel published by Montag Press, following *The Spirit of Laughter* in 2020 and *Carrion* in 2015. His Spanish language novel, *Gato y Lobo*, was published in Mexico City by Wampo in 2022. He has also had numerous short stories published by various online magazines, including the Spadina Literary Review, the Danforth Review and more.

To learn more about Jonathan R. Rose, you can visit his website at www.JonathanRRose.com

www.ingramcontent.com/pod-product-compliance
Lightning Source LLC
Chambersburg PA
CBHW030127260626
47156CB00008B/2827